The Unbidden Guest by E. W. Hornung

Ernest William Hornung was born in Middlesbrough, England on 7th June 1866, the third son and youngest of eight children.

Although spending most of his life in England and France he spent two years in Australia from 1884 and that experience was to colour and influence much of his written works.

His most famous character A. J. Raffles, 'the gentleman thief', was published first in Cassell's Magazine during 1898 and was to make him famous across the world as the new century dawned.

Hornung also wrote several stage plays and was a gifted poet.

Spending time with the troops in WWI he published Notes of a Camp-Follower on the Western Front during 1919, a detailed account of his time there. This was especially close to his heart as his son, and only child, was killed at the Second Battle of Ypres on 6th July 1915.

Ernest William Hornung died in Saint-Jean-de-Luz, in the south of France on 22nd March 1921.

Index of Contents

CHAPTER I

THE GIRL FROM HOME

Arabella was the first at the farm to become aware of Mr. Teesdale's return from Melbourne. She was reading in the parlour, with her plump elbows planted upon the faded green table-cloth, and an untidy head of light-coloured hair between her hands; looking up from her book by chance, she saw through the closed window her father and the buggy climbing the hill at the old mare's own pace. Arabella went on reading until the buggy had drawn up within a few feet of the verandah posts and a few more of the parlour window. Then she sat in doubt, with her finger on the place; but before it appeared absolutely necessary to jump up and run out, one of the men had come up to take charge of the mare, and Arabella was enabled to remove her finger and read on.

The parlour was neither very large nor at all lofty, and the shut window and fire-place closely covered by a green gauze screen, to keep the flies out, made it disagreeably stuffy. There were two doors, but both of these were shut also, though the one at the far end of the room, facing the hearth, nearly always stood wide open. It led down a step into a very little room where the guns were kept and old newspapers thrown, and where somebody was whistling rather sweetly as the other door opened and Mr. Teesdale entered, buggy-whip in hand.

He was a frail, tallish old gentleman, with a venerable forehead, a thin white beard, very little hair to his pate, and clear brown eyes that shone kindly upon all the world. He had on the old tall hat he always wore when driving into Melbourne, and the yellow silk dust-coat which had served him for many a red-hot summer, and was still not unpresentable. Arabella was racing to the end of a paragraph when he entered, and her father had stolen forward and kissed her untidy head before she looked up.

"Bad girl," said he, playfully, "to let your old father get home without ever coming out to meet him!"

"I was trying to finish this chapter," said Arabella. She went on trying.

"I know, I know! I know you of old, my dear. Yet I can't talk, because I am as bad as you are; only I should like to see you reading something better than the Family Cherub." There were better things in the little room adjoining, where behind the shooting lumber was some motley reading, on two long sagging shelves; but that room was known as the gun-room, and half those books were hidden away behind powder-canisters, cartridge-cases, and the like, while all were deep in dust.

"You read it yourself, father," said Arabella as she turned over a leaf of her Family Cherub.

"I read it myself. More shame for me! But then I've read all them books in the little gun-room, and that's what I should like to see you reading now and then. Now why have you got yon door shut, Arabella, and who's that whistling in there?"

"It's our John William," Miss Teesdale said; and even as she spoke the door in question was thrown open by a stalwart fellow in a Crimean shirt, with the sleeves rolled up from arms as brown and hard-looking as mellow oak. He had a breech-loader in one hand and a greasy rag in the other.

"Holloa, father!" cried he, boisterously.

"Well, John William, what are you doing?"

"Cleaning my gun. What have you been doing, that's more like it? What took you trapesing into Melbourne the moment I got my back turned this morning?"

"Why, hasn't your mother told you?"

"Haven't seen her since I came in."

"Well, but Arabella—"

"Arabella! I'm full up of Arabella," said John William contemptuously; but the girl was still too deep in the Family Cherub to heed him. "There's no getting a word out of Arabella when she's on the read; so what's it all about, father?"

"I'll tell you; but you'd better shut yon window, John William, or I don't know what your mother 'll say when she comes in and finds the place full o' flies."

It was the gun-room window that broke the law of no fresh air, causing Mr. Teesdale uneasiness until John William shut it with a grumble; for in this homestead the mistress was law-maker, and indeed master, with man-servant and maid-servant, husband and daughter, and a particularly headstrong son, after her own heart, all under her thumb together.

"Now then, father, what was it took you into Melbourne all of a sudden like that?"

"A letter by the English mail, from my old friend Mr. Oliver."

"Never heard tell of him," said John William, making spectacles of his burnished bores, and looking through them into the sunlight. Already he had lost interest.

Mr. Teesdale was also occupied, having taken from his pocket a very large red cotton handkerchief, with which he was wiping alternately the dust from his tall hat and the perspiration from the forehead whereon the hat had left a fiery rim. Now, however, he nodded his bald head and clicked his lips, as one who gives another up.

"Well, well! Never heard tell of him—you who've heard me tell of him time out o' mind! Nay, come; why, you're called after him yourself! Ay, we called you after John William Oliver because he was the best friend that ever we had in old Yorkshire or anywhere else; the very best; and you pretend you've never heard tell of him."

"What had he got to say for himself?" said Mr. Oliver's namesake, with a final examination of the outside of his barrels.

"Plenty; he's sent one of his daughters out in the Parramatta, that got in with the mail yesterday afternoon; and of course he had given her an introduction to me."

"What's that?" exclaimed John William, looking up sharply, as he ran over the words in his ear. "I say, father, we don't want her here," he added earnestly.

"Oh, did you find out where she was? Have you seen her? What is she like?" cried Arabella, jumping up from the table and joining the others with a face full of questions. She had that instant finished her chapter.

"I don't know what she's like; I didn't see her; I couldn't even find out where she was, though I tried at half a dozen hotels and both coffee-palaces," said the farmer with a crestfallen air.

"All the better!" cried John William, grounding his gun with a bang. "We don't want none of your stuck-up new chums or chumesses here, father."

"I don't know that; for my part, I should love to have a chance of talking to an English young lady," Arabella said, with a backward glance at her Family Cherub. "They're very rich, the Olivers," she added for her brother's benefit; "that's their house in the gilt frame in the best parlour, the house with the tower; and the group in the frame to match, that is the Olivers, isn't it, father?"

"It is, my dear; that's to say, it was, some sixteen years ago. We must get yon group and see which one it is that has come out, and then I'll read you Mr. Oliver's letter, John William. If only he'd written a mail or two before the child started! However, if we've everything made snug for her to-night, I'll lay hands on her to-morrow if she's in Melbourne; and then she shall come out here for a month or two to start with, just to see how she likes it."

"How d'ye know she'll want to come out here at all?" asked John William. "Don't you believe it, father; she wouldn't care for it a little bit."

"Not care for it? Not want to come out and make her home with her parents' old friends? Then she's not her father's daughter," cried Mr. Teesdale indignantly; "she's no child of our good old friends. Why, it was Mr. Oliver who gave me the watch I—hush! Was that your mother calling?"

It was. "David! David! Have you got back, David?" the harsh voice came crying through the lath-and-plaster walls.

Mr. Teesdale scuttled to the door. "Yes, my dear, I've just got in. No, I'm not smoking. Where are you, then? In the spare room? All right, I'm coming, I'm coming." And he was gone.

"Mother's putting the spare room to rights already," Arabella explained.

"I'm sorry to hear it; let's hope it won't be wanted."

"Why, John William? It would be such fun to have a young lady from Home to stay with us!"

"I'm full up o' young ladies, and I'm just sick of the sound of Home. She'll be a deal too grand for us, and there won't be much fun in that. What's the use o' talking? If it was a son of this here old Oliver's it'd be a different thing; we'd precious soon knock the nonsense out of him; I'd undertake to do it myself; but a girl's different, and I jolly well hope she'll stop away. We don't want her here, I tell you. We haven't even invited her. It's a piece of cheek, is the whole thing!"

John William was in the parlour now, sitting on the horse-hair sofa, and laying down the law with freckled fist and blusterous voice, as his habit was. It was a good-humoured sort of bluster, however, and indeed John William seldom opened his mouth without displaying his excellent downright nature in one good light or another. He had inherited his mother's qualities along with her sharp, decided features, which in the son were set off by a strong black beard and bristling moustache. He managed the farm, the men, Arabella, and his father; but all under Mrs. Teesdale, who managed him. Not that this masterful young man was so young in years as you might well suppose; neither John William nor Arabella was under thirty; but their lives had been so simple and so hard-working that, going by their conversation merely, you would have placed the two of them in their teens. For her part, too, Arabella looked much younger than she was, with her wholesome, attractive face and dreamy, inquisitive eyes; and as for the brother, he was but a boy with a beard, still primed with rude health and strength, and still loaded with all the assorted possibilities of budding manhood.

"I've taken down the group," said Mr. Teesdale, returning with a large photograph in a gilt frame; "and here is the letter on the chimney-piece. We'll have a look at them both again."

On the chimney-piece also were the old man's spectacles, which he proceeded to put on, and a tobacco jar and long clay pipe, at which he merely looked lovingly; for Mrs. Teesdale would have no smoking in the house. His own chair stood in the cosy corner between the window and the hearth; and he now proceeded to pull it up to his own place at the head of the table as though it were a meal-time, and that gilt-framed photograph the only dish. Certainly he sat down to it with an appetite never felt during the years it had hung in the unused, ornamental next room, without the least prospect of the Teesdales ever more seeing any member of that group in the flesh. But now that such a prospect was directly at hand, there was some sense in studying the old photograph. It was of eight persons: the parents, a grandparent, and five children. Three of the latter were little girls, in white stockings and hideous boots with low heels and elastic sides; and to the youngest of these three, a fair-haired child whose features, like those of the whole family, were screwed up by a strong light and an exposure of the ancient length, Mr. Teesdale pointed with his finger-nail.

"That's the one," said he. "She now is a young lady of five or six and twenty."

"Don't think much of her looks," observed John William.

"Oh, you can't tell what she may be like from this," Arabella said, justly. "She may be beautiful now; besides, look how the sun must have been in her eyes, poor little thing! What's her name again, father?"

"Miriam, my dear."

"Miriam! I call it a jolly name, don't you, Jack?"

"It's a beast of a name," said John William.

"Stop while I read you a bit of the letter," cried the old man, smiling indulgently. "I won't give you all of it, but just this little bit at the end. He's been telling me that Miriam has her own ideas about things, has already seen something of the world, and isn't perhaps quite like the girls I may remember when we were both young men—"

"Didn't I tell you?" interrupted John William, banging the table with his big fist. "She's stuck-up! We don't want her here."

"But just hark how he ends up. I want you both to listen to these few lines:—'It may even be that she has formed habits and ways which were not the habits and ways of young girls in our day, and that you may like some of these no better than I do. Yet her heart, my dear Teesdale, is as pure and as innocent as her mother's was before her, and I know that my old friend will let no mere modern mannerisms prejudice him against my darling child, who is going so far from us all. It has been a rather sudden arrangement, and though the doctors ordered it, and Miriam can take care of herself as only the girls nowadays can, still I would never have parted with her had I not known of one tried friend to meet and welcome her at the other end. Keep her at your station, my dear Teesdale, as long as you can, for an open-air life is, I am convinced, what she wants above all things. If she should need money, an accident which may always happen, let her have whatever she wants, advising me of the amount immediately. I have told her to apply to you in such an extremity, which, however, I regard as very unlikely to occur. I have also provided her with a little note of introduction, with which she will find her way to you as soon as possible after landing. And into your kind old hands, and those of your warm-hearted wife, I cheerfully commend my girl, with the most affectionate remembrances to you both, and only regretting that business will not allow me to come out with her and see you both once more.' Then he finishes— calls himself my affectionate friend, same as when we were boys together. And it's two-and-thirty years since we said good-bye!" added Mr. Teesdale as he folded up the letter and put it away.

He pushed his spectacles on to his forehead, for they were dim, and sat gazing straight ahead, through the inner door that stood now wide open, and out of the gun-room window. This overlooked a sunburnt decline, finishing, perhaps a furlong from the house, at the crests of the river timber, that stood out of it like a hedge, by reason of the very deep cut made by the Yarra, where it formed the farm boundary on that side. And across the top of the window (to one sitting in Mr. Teesdale's place) was stretched, like a faded mauve ribbon, a strip of the distant Dandenong Ranges; and this and the timber were the favourite haunts of the old man's eyes, for thither they strayed of their own accord whenever his mind got absent elsewhere, as was continually happening, and had happened now.

"It's a beautiful letter!" exclaimed Arabella warmly.

"I like it, too," John William admitted; "but I shan't like the girl. That kind don't suit me at all; but I'll try to be civil to her on account of the old man, for his letter is right enough."

Mr. Teesdale looked pleased, though he left his eyes where they were.

"Ay, ay, my dears, I thought you would like it. Ah, but all his letters are the same! Two-and-thirty years, and never a year without at least three letters from Mr. Oliver. He's a business man, and he always answers promptly. He's a rich man now, my dears, but he doesn't forget the early friends, not he, though they're at the other end of the earth, and as poor as he's rich."

"Yet he doesn't seem to know how we're situated, for all that," remarked John William thoughtfully. "Look how he talks about our 'station,' and of your advancing money to the girl, as though we were rolling in it like him! Have you never told him our circumstances, father?"

At the question, Mr. Teesdale's eyes fell twenty miles, and rested guiltily upon the old green tablecloth.

"I doubt a station and a farm convey much the same thing in the old country," he answered crookedly.

"That you may bet they do!" cried the son, with a laugh; but he went on delivering himself of the most discouraging prophecies touching the case in point. The girl would come out with false ideas; would prove too fine by half for plain people like themselves; and at the best was certain to expect much more than they could possibly give her.

"Well, as to that," said the farmer, who thought himself lucky to have escaped a scolding for never having told an old friend how poor he was—"as to that, we can but give her the best we've got, with mebbe a little extra here and there, such as we wouldn't have if we were by ourselves. The eggs 'll be fresh, at any rate, and I think that she'll like her sheets, for your mother is getting out them 'at we brought with us from Home in '51. There was just two pairs, and she's had 'em laid by in lavender ever since. We can give her a good cup o' tea, an' all; and you can take her out 'possum-shooting, John William, and teach her how to ride. Yes, we'll make a regular bush-girl of her in a month, and send her back to Yorkshire the picture of health; though as yet I'm not very clear what's been the matter with her. But if she takes after her parents ever so little she'll see that we're doing our best, and that'll be good enough for any child of theirs."

From such a shabby waistcoat pocket Mr. Tees-dale took so handsome a gold watch, it was like a ring on a beggar's finger; and he fondled it between his worn hands, but without a word.

"Mr. Oliver gave you that watch, didn't he, father?" Arabella said, watching him.

"He did, my dear," said the old man proudly. "He came and saw us off at the Docks, and he gave me the watch on board, just as we were saying good-bye; and he gave your mother a gold brooch which neither of you have ever seen, for I've never known her wear it myself."

Arabella said she had seen it.

"Now his watch," continued Mr. Teesdale, "has hardly ever left my pocket—save to go under my pillow—since he put it in my hands on July 3, 1851. Here's the date and our initials inside the case; but you've seen them before. Ay, but there are few who came out in '51—and stopped out—who have done as poorly as me. The day after we dropped anchor in Hobson's Bay there wasn't a living soul aboard our ship; captain, mates, passengers and crew, all gone to the diggings. Every man Jack but me! It was just before you were born, John William, and I wasn't going. It may have been a mistake, but the Lord knows best. To be sure, we had our hard times when the diggers were coming into Melbourne and shoeing their horses with gold, and filling buckets with champagne, and standing by with a pannikin to make everybody drink that passed; if you wouldn't, you'd got to take off your coat and show why. I remember one of them offering me a hundred pounds for this very watch, and precious hard up I was, but I wouldn't take it, not I, though I didn't refuse a sovereign for telling him the time. Ay, sovereigns were the pennies of them days; not that I fingered many; but I never got so poor as to part with Mr. Oliver's watch, and you never must either, John William, when it's yours. Ay, ay," chuckled Mr. Teesdale, as he snapped-to the case and replaced the watch in his pocket, "and it's gone like a book for over thirty years, with nothing worse than a cleaning the whole time."

"You must mind and tell that to Miriam, father," said Arabella, smiling.

"I must so. Ah, my dear, I shall have two daughters, not one, and you'll have a sister while Miriam is here."

"That depends what Miriam is like," said John William, getting up from the sofa with a Hugh and going back idly to the little room and his cleaned gun.

"I know what she will be like," said Arabella, placing the group in front of her on the table. "She will be delicate and fair, and rather small; and I shall have to show her everything, and take tremendous care of her."

"I wonder if she'll have her mother's hazel eyes and gentle voice?" mused the farmer aloud, with his eyes on their way back to the Dandenong Ranges.

"I should like her to take after her mother; she was one of the gentlest little women that ever I knew, was Mrs. Oliver, and I never clapped eyes—"

The speaker suddenly turned his head; there had been a step in the verandah, and some person had passed the window too quick for recognition.

"Who was that?" said Mr. Teesdale.

"I hardly saw," said Arabella, pushing back her chair. "It was a woman."

"And now she's knocking! Run and see who it is, my dear."

Arabella rose and ran. Then followed such an outcry in the passage that Mr. Teesdale rose also. He was on his legs in time to see the door flung wide open, and the excited eyes of Arabella reaching over the shoulder of the tall young woman whom she was pushing into the room.

"Here is Miriam," she cried. "Here's Miriam found her way out all by herself!"

CHAPTER II

A BAD BEGINNING

At the sound of the voices outside, John William, for his part, had slipped behind the gun-room door; but he had the presence of mind not to shut it quite, and this enabled him to peer through the crack and take deliberate stock of the fair visitant.

She was a well-built young woman, with a bold, free carriage and a very daring smile. That was John William's first impression when he came to think of it in words a little later. His eyes then fastened upon her hair. The poor colour of her face and lips did not strike him at the time any more than the smudges under the merry eyes. The common stamp of the regular features never struck him at all, for of such matters old Mr. Teesdale himself was hardly a judge; but the girl's hair took John William's fancy on the spot. It was the most wonderful hair: red, and yet beautiful. There was plenty of it to be seen, too, for the straw hat that hid the rest had a backward tilt to it, while an exuberant fringe came down within an inch of the light eyebrows. John William could have borne it lower still. He watched and listened with a smile upon his own hairy visage, of which he was totally unaware.

"So this is my old friend's daughter!" the farmer had cried out.

"And you're Mr. Scarsdale, are you?" answered the girl, between fits of intermittent, almost hysterical laughter.

"Eh? Yes, yes; I'm Mr. Teesdale, and this is my daughter Arabella. You are to be sisters, you two."

The visitor turned to Arabella and gave her a sounding kiss upon the lips.

"And mayn't I have one too?" old Teesdale asked. "I'm that glad to see you, my dear, and you know you're to look upon me like a father as long as you stay in Australia. Thank you, Miriam. Now I feel as if you'd been here a week already!"

Mr. Teesdale had received as prompt and as hearty a kiss as his daughter before him.

"Mrs. Teesdale is busy, but she'll come directly," he went on to explain. "Do you know what she's doing? She's getting your room ready, Miriam. We knew that you had landed, and I've spent the whole day hunting for you in town. Just to think that you should have come out by yourself after all! But our John William was here a minute ago. John William, what are you doing?"

"Cleaning my gun," said the young man, coming from behind his door, greasy rag in hand.

"Nay, come! You finished that job long ago. Come and shake hands with Miriam. Look, here she is, safe and sound, and come out all by herself!"

"I'm very glad to see you," said the son of the house, advancing, dirty palms foremost, "but I'm sorry I can't shake hands!"

"Then I'd better kiss you too!"

She had taken a swinging step forward, and the red fringe was within a foot of his startled face, when she tossed back her head with a hearty laugh.

"No, I think I won't. You're too old and you're not old enough—see?"

"John William 'll be three-and-thirty come January," said Mr. Teesdale gratuitously.

"Yes? That's ten years older than me," answered the visitor with equal candour. "Exactly ten!"

"Nay, come—not exactly ten," the old gentleman said, with some gravity, for he was a great stickler for the literal truth; "only seven or eight, I understood from your father?"

The visitor coloured, then pouted, and then burst out laughing as she exclaimed, "You oughtn't to be so particular about ladies' ages! Surely two or three years is near enough, isn't it? I'm ashamed of you, Mr. Teesdale; I really am!" And David received such a glance that he became exceedingly ashamed of himself; but the smile that followed it warmed his old heart through and through, and reminded him, he thought, of Miriam's mother.

Meantime, the younger Teesdale remained rooted to the spot where he had been very nearly kissed. He was still sufficiently abashed, but perhaps on that very account a plain speech came from him too.

"You're not like what I expected. No, I'm bothered if you are!"

"Much worse?" asked the girl, with a scared look.

"No, much better. Ten thousand times better!" cried the young man. Then his shyness overtook him, and, though he joined in the general laughter, he ventured no further remarks. As to the laughter, the visitor's was the most infectious ever heard in the weather-board farmhouse. Arabella shook within the comfortable covering with which nature had upholstered her, and old David had to apply the large red handkerchief to his furrowed cheeks before he could give her the message to Mrs. Teesdale, for which there had not been a moment to spare out of the crowded minute or two which had elapsed since the visitor's unforeseen arrival.

"Go, my dear," he said now, "and tell your mother that Miriam is here. That's it. Mrs. T. will be with us directly, Miriam. Ah, I thought this photograph'd catch your eye sooner or later. You'll have seen it once or twice before, eh? Just once or twice, I'm thinking." The group still lay on the table at Mr. Teesdale's end.

"Who are they?" asked the visitor, very carelessly; indeed, she had but given the photograph a glance, and that from a distance.

"Who? Why, yourselves; your own family. All the lot of you when you were little," cried David, snatching up the picture and handing it across. "We were just looking at it when you came, Miriam; and I made you out to be this one, look—this poor little thing with the sun in her eyes."

The old man was pointing with his finger, the girl examining closely. Their heads were together. Suddenly she raised hers, looked him in the eyes, and burst out laughing.

"How clever you are!" she said. "I'm not a bit like that now, now am I?"

She made him look well at her before answering. And in all his after knowledge of it, he never again saw quite so bold and dibonnaire an expression upon that cool face framed in so much hot hair. But from a mistaken sense of politeness, Mr. Teesdale made a disingenuous answer after all, and the subject of conversation veered from the girl who had come out to Australia to those she had left behind her in the old country.

That conversation would recur to Mr. Teesdale in after days. It contained surprises for him at the time. Later, he ceased to wonder at what he had heard. Indeed, there was nothing wonderful in his having nourished quite a number of misconceptions concerning a family of whom he had set eyes on no member for upwards of thirty years. It was those misconceptions which the red-haired member of that family now removed. They were all very natural in the circumstances. And yet, to give an instance, Mr. Teesdale was momentarily startled to ascertain that Mrs. Oliver had never been so well in her life as when her daughter sailed. He had understood from Mr. Oliver that his wife was in a very serious state with diabetes. When he now said so, the innocent remark made Miss Oliver to blush and bite her lips. Then she explained. Her mother had been threatened with the disease in question, but that was all. The real fact was, her father was morbidly anxious about her mother, and to such an extent that it appeared the anxiety amounted to mania.

She put it in her own way.

"Pa's mad on ma," she said. "You can't believe a word he says about her."

Mr. Teesdale found this difficult to believe of his old friend, who seemed to him to write so sensibly about the matter. It made him look out of the gun-room window. Then he recollected that the girl herself lacked health, for which cause she had come abroad.

"And what was the matter with you, Miriam," said he, "for your father only says that the doctors recommended the voyage?"

"Oh, that's all he said, was it?"

"Yes, that's all."

"And you want to know what was the matter with me, do you?"

"No, I was only wondering. It's no business of mine."

"Oh, but I'll tell you. Bless your life, I'm not ashamed of it. It was late nights—it was late nights that was the matter with me."

"Nay, come," cried the farmer; yet, as he peered through his spectacles into the bright eyes sheltered by the fiery fringe, he surmised a deep-lying heaviness in the brain behind them; and he noticed now for the first time how pale a face they were set in, and how gray the marks were underneath them.

"The voyage hasn't done you much good, either," he said. "Why, you aren't even sunburnt."

"No? Well, you see, I'm such a bad sailor. I spent all my time in the cabin, that's how it was."

"Yet the Argus says you had such a good voyage?"

"Yes? I expect they always say that. It was a beast of a voyage, if you ask me, and quite as bad as late nights for you, though not nearly so nice."

"Ah, well, we'll soon set you up, my dear. This is the place to make a good job of you, if ever there was one. But where have you been staying since you landed, Miriam? It's upwards of twenty-four hours now."

The guest smiled.

"Ah, that's tellings. With some people who came out with me—some swells that I knew in the West End, if you particularly want to know; not that I'm much nuts on 'em, either."

"Don't you be inquisitive, father," broke in John William from the sofa. It was his first remark since he had sat down.

"Well, perhaps I mustn't bother you with any more questions now," said Mr. Teesdale to the girl; "but I shall have a hundred to ask you later on. To think that you're Mr. Oliver's daughter after all! Ay, and I see a look of your mother and all now and then. They did well to send you out to us, and get you right away from them late hours and that nasty society—though here comes one that'll want you to tell her all about that by-and-by."

The person in question was Arabella, who had just re-entered.

"Society?" said she. "My word, yes, I shall want you to tell me all about society, Miriam."

"Do you hear that, Miriam?" said Mr. Teesdale after some moments. She had taken no notice.

"What's that? Oh yes, I heard; but I shan't tell anybody anything more unless you all stop calling me Miriam."

This surprised them; it had the air of a sudden thought as suddenly spoken.

"But Miriam's your name," said Arabella, laughing.

"Your father has never spoken of you as anything else," remarked Mr. Teesdale.

"All the same, I'm not used to being called by it," replied their visitor, who for the first time was exhibiting signs of confusion. "I like people to call me what I'm accustomed to being called. You may say it's a pet name, but it's what I'm used to, and I like it best."

"What is, missy?" said old Teesdale kindly; for the girl was staring absently at the opposite wall.

"Tell us, and we'll call you nothing else," Arabella promised.

The girl suddenly swept her eyes from the wall to Mr. Teesdale's inquiring face. "You said it just now," she told him, with a nod and her brightest smile. "You said it without knowing when you called me 'Missy.' That's what they always call me at home—Missy or the Miss. You pays your money and you takes your choice."

"Then I choose Missy," said Arabella. "And now, father, I came with a message from my mother; she wants you to take Missy out into the verandah while we get the tea ready. She wasn't tidy enough to come and see you at once, Missy, but she sends you her love to go on with, and she hopes that you'll excuse her."

"Of course she will," answered Mr. Teesdale for the girl; "but will you excuse me, Missy, if I bring my pipe out with me? I'm just wearying for a smoke."

"Excuse you?" cried Missy, taking the old man's arm as she accompanied him to the door. "Why, bless your life, I love a smoke myself."

John William had jumped up to follow them; had hesitated; and was left behind.

"There!" said Arabella, turning a shocked face upon him the instant they were quite alone.

"She was joking," said John William.

"I don't think it."

"Then you must be a fool, Arabella. Of course she was only in fun."

"But she said so many queer things; and oh, John William, she seems to me so queer altogether!"

"Well, what the deuce did you expect?" cried the other in a temper. "Didn't her own father say that she was something out of the common? What do you know about it, anyway? What do you know about 'modern mannerisms'. Didn't her own father let on that she had some? Even if she did smoke, I shouldn't be surprised or think anything of it; depend upon it they smoke in society, whether they do or they don't in your rotten Family Cherub. But she was only joking when she said that; and I never saw the like of you, Arabella, not to know a joke when you hear one." And John William stamped away to his room; to reappear in a white shirt and his drab tweed suit, exactly as though he had been going into Melbourne for the day.

It was Mrs. Teesdale, perhaps, who put this measure into her son's head; for, as he quitted the parlour, she pushed past him to enter it, in the act of fastening the final buttons of her gray-stuff chapel-going bodice. "Now, then, Arabella," she cried sharply, "let blind down and get them things off table." And on to it, as she spoke, Mrs. Teesdale flung a clean white folded table-cloth which she had carried between elbow and ribs while busy buttoning her dress. As for Arabella, she obeyed each order instantly, displaying an amount of bustling activity which only showed itself on occasions when her mother was particularly hot and irritable; the present was one.

Mrs. Teesdale was a tall, strong woman who at sixty struck one first of all with her strength, activity, and hard, solid pluck. Her courage and her hardness too were written in every wrinkle of a bloodless, weather-beaten face that must have been sharp and pointed even in girlhood; and those same dominant qualities shone continually in a pair of eyes like cold steel—the eyes of a woman who had never given in. The woman had not her husband's heart full of sympathy and affection for all but the very worst who came his way. She had neither his moderately good education, nor his immoderately ready and helping hand even for the worst. Least of all had she his simple but adequate sense of humour; of this quality and all its illuminating satellites Mrs. Teesdale was totally devoid. Yet, but for his wife, old David would probably have found himself facing his latter end in one or other of the Benevolent Asylums of that Colony; whereas with the wife's character inside the husband's skin, it is not improbable that the name of David Teesdale would have been known and honoured in the land where his days had been long indeed, but sadly unprofitable.

Arabella, then, who had inherited some of David's weak points, just as John William possessed his mother's strong ones, could work with the best of them when she liked and Mrs. Teesdale drove. In ten minutes the tea was ready; and it was a more elaborate tea than usual, for there was quince jam as well as honey, and, by great good luck, cold boiled ham in addition to hot boiled eggs. Last of all, John William, when he was ready, picked a posy of geraniums from the bed outside the gun-room outer door (which was invisible from the verandah, where David and the visitor could be heard chatting), and placed them in the centre of the clean table-cloth. Then Mrs. Teesdale drew up the blind; and a nice sight met their eyes.

Mr. Teesdale was discovered in earnest expostulation with the girl from England, who was smoking his pipe. She had jumped on to the wooden armchair upon which, a moment ago, she had no doubt been seated; now she was dancing upon it, slowly and rhythmically, from one foot to the other, and while holding the long clay well above the old man's reach, she kept puffing at it with such immense energy that the smoke hung in a cloud about her rakish fringe and wicked smile, under the verandah slates. A smile flickered also across the entreating face of David Teesdale; and it was this his unpardonable show of taking the outrage in good part, that made away with the wife's modicum of self-control. Doubling a hard-working fist, she was on the point of knocking at the window with all the might that it would bear, when her wrist was held and the blind let down. And it was John William who faced her indignation with the firm front which she herself had given him.

"I am very sorry, mother," said he quietly, "but you are not going to make a scene."

Such was the power of Mrs. Teesdale in her own home, she could scarcely credit her hearing. "Not going to?" she cried, for the words had been tuned neither to question nor entreaty, but a command. "Let go my hands this moment, sir!"

"Then don't knock," said John William, complying; and there was never a knock; but the woman was blazing.

"How dare you?" she said; and indeed, man and boy, he had never dared so much before.

"You were going to make a scene," said he, as kindly as ever; "and though we didn't invite her, she is our guest—"

"You may be ashamed of yourself! I don't care who she is; she shan't smoke here."

"She is also the daughter of your oldest friends; and hasn't her own father written to say she has ways and habits which the girls hadn't when you were one? Not that smoking's a habit of hers: not likely. I'll bet she's only done this for a lark. And you're to say nothing more about it, mother, do you see?"

"Draw up the blind," said Mrs. Teesdale, speaking to her son as she had spoken to him all his life, but, for the first time, without confidence. "Draw up the blind, and disobey me at your peril."

"Then promise to say nothing about it to the girl."

They eyed each other for a minute. In the end the mother said: "To the girl? No, of course I won't say anything to her—unless it happens again." It was not even happening when the blind was drawn up, and it never did happen again. But Mrs. Teesdale had given in, for once in her life, and to one of her own children. Moreover, there was an alien in the case, who was also a girl; and this was the beginning between these three.

CHAPTER III

It was not a very good beginning, and the first to feel that was John William himself. He felt it at tea. During the meal his mouth never opened, except on business; but his eyes made up for it.

He saw everything. He saw that his mother and Missy would never get on; he knew it the moment they kissed. There was no sounding smack that time. The visitor, for her part, seemed anxious to show that even she could be shy if she tried; and as for Mrs. Teesdale and her warm greeting, it was very badly done. The tone was peevish, and her son, for one, could hear between the words. "You're our old friends' child," he heard her saying in her heart, "but I don't think I shall like you; for you've come without letting me know, you've smoked, and you've set my own son against me—already." He was half sorry that he had checked, what is as necessary to some as the breath they draw, a little plain speaking at the outset. But sooner or later, about one thing or another, this was bound to come; and come it did.

"I can't think, Miriam," said Mrs. Teesdale, "how you came by that red hair o' yours! Your father's was very near black, and your mother's a light brown wi' a streak o' gold in it; but there wasn't a red hair in either o' their heads that I can remember."

At this speech John William bit off an oath under his beard, while David looked miserably at his wife, and Arabella at their visitor, who first turned as red as her hair, and then burst into a fit of her merriest laughter.

"Well, I can't help it, can I?" cried she, with a good-nature that won two hearts, at any rate. "I didn't choose my hair; it grew its own colour—all I've got to do is to keep it on!"

"Yes, but it's that red!" exclaimed Mrs. Teesdale stolidly, while John William chuckled and looked less savage.

"Ah, you could light your old pipe at it," said Missy to the farmer, making the chuckler laugh outright.

Not so Mr. Teesdale. "My dear," he said to his wife; "my dear!"

"Well, but I could understand it, David, if her parents' hairs had any red in 'em. In the only photograph we have of you, Miriam, which is that group there taken when you were all little, you look to have your mother's fair hair. I can't make it out."

"No?" said Missy, sweetly. "Then you didn't know that red always comes out light in a photograph?"

"Oh, I know nothing at all about that," said Mrs. Teesdale, with the proper disregard for a lost point. "Then have the others all got red hair too?"

"N—no, I'm the only one."

"Well, that's a good thing, Miriam, I'm sure it is!"

"Nay, come, my dear, that'll do," whispered David; while John William said loudly, to change the subject, "You're not to call her Miriam, mother."

"And why not, I wonder?"

"Because she's not used to it. She says they call her Missy at home; and we want to make her at home here, surely to goodness!"

Missy had smiled gratefully on John William and nodded confirmation of his statement to Mrs. Teesdale, who, however, shook her head.

"Ay, but I don't care for nicknames at all," said she, without the shadow of a smile; "I never did and I never shall, John William. So, Miriam, you'll have to put up with your proper name from me, for I'm too old to change. And I'm sure it's not an ugly one," added the dour woman, less harshly. "Is your cup off, Miriam?" she added to that; she did not mean to be quite as she was.

It was at this point, however, that the visitor asked Mr. Teesdale the time, and that Mr. Teesdale, with a sudden eloquence in his kind old eyes, showed her the watch which Mr. Oliver had given him; speaking most touchingly of her father's goodness, and kindness, and generosity, and of their lifelong friendship. Thus the long hand marked some minutes while the watch was still out before it appeared why Missy wanted to know the time. She then declared she must get back to Melbourne before dark, a statement which provoked some brisk opposition, notably on the part of Mr. Teesdale. But the girl showed commendable firmness. She would go back as she had come, by the six o'clock 'bus from the township. None of them, however, would hear of the 'bus, and John William waited until a compromise had been effected by her giving way on this point; then he went out to put-to.

This proved a business. The old mare had already made one journey into Melbourne and back; and that was some nine miles each way. There was another buggy-horse, but it had to be run up from the paddock. Thus twenty minutes elapsed before John William led horse and trap round to the front of the house. He found the party he had left mildly arguing round the tea-table, now assembled on the grass below the red-brick verandah. They were arguing still, it seemed, and not quite so mildly. Missy was buttoning a yellow glove, the worse for wear, and she was standing like a rock, with her mouth shut tight. Mr. Teesdale had on his tall hat and his dust-coat, and the whip was once more in his hand; at the sight of him his son's heel went an inch into the ground.

"Only fancy!" cried the old man in explanation. "She says she's not coming back to us any more. She doesn't want to come out and stay with us!"

Arabella echoed the "Only fancy!" while Mrs. Teesdale thought of the old folks who had been young when she was, and said decisively, "But she'll have to."

John William said nothing at all; but it was to him the visitor now looked appealingly.

"It isn't that I shouldn't like it—that isn't it at all—it's that you wouldn't like me! Oh, you don't know what I am. You don't, I tell you straight. I'm not fit to come and stay here—I should put you all about so—there's no saying what I shouldn't do. You can't think how glad I am to have seen you all. It's a jolly old place, and I shall be able to tell 'em all at home just what it's like. But you'd far better let me rest where I am—you—you—you really had."

She had given way, not to tears, indeed, but to the slightly hysterical laughter which had characterised her entry into the parlour when John William was looking through the crack. Now she once more made her laughter loud, and it seemed particularly inconsequent. Yet here was a sign of irresolution which old David, as the wisest of the Teesdales, was the first to recognise. Moreover, her eyes were flying from the weather-board farmhouse to the river timber down the hill, from the soft cool grass to the peaceful sky, and from hay-stack to hen-yard, as though the whole simple scene were a temptation to her; and David saw this also.

"Nonsense," said he firmly; and to the others, "She'll come back and stay with us till she's tired of us— we'll never be tired of you, Missy. Ay, of course she will. You leave her to me, Mrs. T."

"Then," said Missy, snatching her eyes from their last fascination, a wattle-bush in bloom, "will you take all the blame if I turn out a bad egg?"

"A what?" said Mrs. Teesdale.

"Of course we will," cried her husband, turning a deaf ear to John William, who was trying to speak to him.

"You promise, all of you!"

"Of course we do," answered the farmer again; but he had not answered John William.

"Then I'll come, and your blood be on your own heads."

For a moment she stood smiling at them all in turn; and not a soul of them saw her next going without thinking of this one. The low sun struck full upon the heavy red fringe, and on the pale face and the devil-may-care smile which it over-hung just then. At the back of that smile there was a something which seemed to be coming up swiftly like a squall at sea; but only for one moment; the next, she had kissed the women, shaken hands with the young man, mounted into the buggy beside Mr. Teesdale, and the two of them were driving slowly down the slope.

"I think, John William," said his mother, "that you might have driven in this time, instead o' letting your father go twice."

"Didn't I want to?" replied John William, in a bellow which made Missy turn her head at thirty yards. "He was bent on going. He's the most pig-headed old man in the Colony. He wouldn't even answer me when I spoke to him about it just now."

He turned on his heel, and mother and daughter were at last alone, and free to criticise.

"For a young lady fresh from England," began the former, "I must say I thought it was a shabby dress— didn't you?"

"Shabby isn't the word," said Arabella; "if you ask me, I call her whole style flashy—as flashy as it can stick."

CHAPTER IV

A MATTER OF TWENTY POUNDS

This is jolly!" exclaimed Missy, settling herself comfortably at the old man's side as she handed him back the reins. They had just jogged out of the lowest paddock, and Mr. Teesdale had been down to remove the slip-rails and to replace them after Missy had driven through.

"Very nicely done," the farmer said, in his playful, kindly fashion. "I see you've handled the ribbons before."

"Never in my life!"

"Indeed? I should have thought that with all them horses and carriages every one of you would have learnt to ride and drive."

"Yes, you would think so," Missy said, after a pause; "but in my case you'd think wrong. I can't bear horses, so I tell you straight. One flew at me when I was a little girl, and I've never gone near 'em since."

"Flew at you!" exclaimed Mr. Teesdale. "Nay, come!"

"Well, you know what I mean. I'd show you the bite—"

"Oh, it bit you? Now I see, now I see."

"You saw all along!"

"No, it was such a funny way of putting it."

"You knew what I meant," persisted Missy. "If you're going to make game of me, I'll get down and walk. Shall we be back in Melbourne by seven?"

Mr. Teesdale drew out his watch with a proud smile and a tender hand. He loved consulting it before anybody, but Missy's presence gave the act a special charm. He shook his head, however, in answer to her question.

"We'll not do it," said he; "it's ten past six already."

"Then how long is it going to take us?"

"Well, not much under the hour; you see—"

A groan at his side made Mr. Teesdale look quickly round; and there was trouble under the heavy fringe.

"I must be there soon after seven!" cried the girl petulantly.

"Ay, but where, Missy? I'll do my best," said David, snatching up the whip, "if you'll tell me where it is you want to be."

"It's the Bijou Theatre—I'm supposed to be there by seven—to meet the people I'm staying with, you know."

David had begun to use the whip vigorously, but now he hesitated and looked pained. "I am sorry to hear it's a theatre you want to get to," said he gravely.

"Why, do you think them such sinks of iniquity—is that it?" asked the girl, laughing.

"I never was in a theatre in my life, Missy; I don't approve of them, my dear."

"No more do I—no more do I! But when you're staying with people you can't always be your own boss, now can you?"

"You could with us, Missy."

"Well, that's bully; but I can't with these folks. They're regular terrors for the theatre, the folks I'm staying with now, and I don't know what they'll say if I keep 'em waiting long. Think you can do it?"

"Not by seven; but I think we might get there between five and ten minutes past."

"Thank God!"

Mr. Teesdale wrinkled his forehead, but said nothing. Evidently it was of the first importance that Missy should not keep her friends waiting. Of these people, however, she had already spoken so lightly that David was pleased to fancy her as not caring very much about them. He was pleased, not only because they took her to the theatre, but because he wanted no rival Australian friends for his old friend's child; the farm, if possible, must be her only home so long as she remained in the Colony. When, therefore, the girl herself confirmed his hopes the very next time she opened her mouth, the old man beamed with satisfaction.

"These folks I'm staying with," said Missy—"I'm not what you call dead nuts on 'em, as I said before."

"I'm glad to hear it," chuckled David, "because we want you all to ourselves, my dear."

"So you think! Some day you'll be sorry you spoke."

"Nonsense, child. What makes you talk such rubbish? You've got to come and make your home with us until you're tired of us, as I've told you already. Where is it they live, these friends of yours?"

"Where do they live?" repeated Missy. "Oh, in Kew."

"Ah—Kew."

The name was spoken in a queer, noticeable tone, as of philosophic reflection. Then the farmer smiled and went on driving in silence; they were progressing at a good speed now. But Missy had looked up anxiously.

"What do you know about Kew?" said she.

"Not much," replied David, with a laugh; "only once upon a time I had a chance of buying it—and had the money too!"

"You had the money to buy Kew?"

"Yes, I had it. There was a man who took me on to a hill and showed me a hollow full of scrub and offered to get me the refusal of it for an old song. I had the money and all, as it happened, but I wasn't going to throw it away. The place looked a howling wilderness; but it is now the suburb of Kew."

"Think of that. Aren't you sorry you didn't buy it?"

"Oh, it makes no difference."

"But you'd be so rich if you had!"

"I should be a millionaire twice over," said the farmer, complacently, as he removed his ruin of a top-hat to let in the breeze upon his venerable pate. Missy sat aghast at him.

"It makes me sick to think of it," she exclaimed. "I don't know what I couldn't do to you! If I'd been you I'd have cut my throat years ago. To think of the high old time you could have had!"

"I never had that much desire for a high old time," said Mr. Teesdale with gentle exaltation.

"Haven't I, then, that's all!" cried his companion in considerable excitement. "It makes a poor girl feel bad to hear you go on like that."

"But you're not a poor girl."

Missy was silenced.

"Yes, I am," she said at last, with an air of resolution. It was not, however, until they were the better part of a mile nearer Melbourne.

"You are what?"

"A poor girl."

"Nonsense, my dear. I wonder what your father would say if he heard you talk like that."

"He's got nothing to do with it."

"Not when he's worth thousands, Missy?"

"Not when he's thousands of miles away, Mr. Teesdale."

Mr. Teesdale raised his wrinkled forehead and drove on. A look of mingled anxiety and pain aged him years in a minute. Soon the country roads were left behind, and the houses began closing up on either side of a very long and broad high road. It was ten minutes to seven by Mr. Teesdale's watch when he looked at it again. It was time for him to say the difficult thing which had occurred to him two or three miles back, and he said it in the gentlest tones imaginable from an old man of nearly seventy.

"Missy, my dear, is it possible" (so he put it) "that you have run short of the needful?"

"It's a fact," said Missy light-heartedly.

"But how, my dear, have you managed to do that?"

"How? Let's see. I gave a lot away—to a woman in the steerage—whose husband went and died at sea. He died of dropsy. I nursed him, I did. Rather! I helped lay him out when he was dead. But don't go telling anybody—please."

Mr. Teesdale had shuddered uncontrollably; now, however, he shifted the reins to his right hand in order to pat Missy with his left.

"You're a noble girl. You are that! Yet it's only what I should have expected of their child. I might ha' known you'd be a noble girl."

"But you won't tell anybody?"

"Not if you'd rather I didn't. That proves your nobility! About how much would you like, my dear, to go on with?"

"Oh, twenty pounds."

Mr. Teesdale drew the breeze in through the broken ranks of his teeth.

"Wouldn't—wouldn't ten do, my dear?"

"Ten? Let's think. No, I don't think I could do with a penny less than twenty. You see, a wave came into the cabin and spoilt all my things. I want everything new."

"But I understood you had such a good voyage, Missy?"

"Not from me you didn't! Besides, it was my own fault: I gone and left the window open, and in came a sea. Didn't the captain kick up a shine! But I told him it was worse for me than for him; and look at the old duds I've got to go about in all because! Why, I look quite common—I know I do. No; I must have new before I come out to stay at the farm."

"I'm sure our Arabella dresses simple," the farmer was beginning; but Missy cut him short, and there was a spot of anger on each of her pale cheeks as she broke out:

"But this ain't simple—it's common! I had to borrow the most of it. All my things were spoilt. I can't get a new rig-out for less than twenty pounds, and without everything new—"

"Nay, come!" cried old David, in some trouble. "Of course I'll let you have anything you want—I have your father's instructions to do so. But—but there are difficulties. It's difficult at this moment. You see the banks are closed, and—and—"

"Oh, don't you be in any hurry. Send it when you can; then I'll get the things and come out afterwards. Why, here we are at Lonsdale Street!"

"But I want you to come out soon. How long would it take you to get everything?"

"To-day's Thursday. If I had it to-morrow I could come out on Monday."

"Then you shall have it to-morrow," said David, closing his lips firmly. "Though the banks are closed, there's the man we send our milk to, and he owes me a lump more than twenty pound. I'll go to him now and get the twenty from him, or I'll know the reason why! Yes, and I'll post it to you before I go back home at all! What address must I send it to, Missy?"

"What address? Oh, to the General Post Office. I don't want the folks I am staying with to know. They offered to lend me, and I wouldn't. Will you stop, please?"

"Quite right, my dear, quite right. I was the one to come to. You'll find it at the—"

"Do you mind stopping?"

"Why, we're not there yet. We're not even in Bourke Street."

"No, but please stop here."

"Very well. Here we are, then, and it's only six past. But why not drive right on to the theatre—that's what I want to know?"

Missy hesitated, and hesitated, until she saw the old man peering into her face through the darkness that seemed to have fallen during the last five minutes. Then she dropped her eyes. They had pulled up alongside the deep-cut channel between road-metal and curb-stone, whereby you shall remember the streets of Melbourne. Nobody appeared to be taking any notice of them.

"I see," said David very gently. "And I don't wonder at it. No, Missy, it's not at all the sort of turn-out for your friends to see you in. Jump down, my dear, and I'll just drive alongside to see that nothing happens you. But I won't seem to know you, Missy—I won't seem to know you!"

Lower and lower, as the old man spoke, the girl had been hanging her head; until now he could see nothing of her face on account of her fringe; when suddenly she raised it and kissed his cheek. She was out of the buggy next moment.

She walked at a great rate, but David kept up with her by trotting his horse, and they exchanged signals the whole way. Close to the theatre she beckoned to him to pull up again. He did so, and she came to the wheel with one of her queer, inscrutable smiles.

"How do you know," said she, "that I'm Miriam Oliver at all?"

The rays from a gas-lamp cut between their faces as she looked him full in the eyes.

"Why, of course you are!"

"But how do you know?"

"Nay, come, what a question! What makes you ask it, Missy?"

"Because I've given you no proof. I brought an introduction with me and I went and forgot to give it to you. However, here it is, so you may as well put it in your pipe and smoke it."

She took some letters out of her pocket as she spoke, and shifted the top one to the bottom until she came to an envelope that had never been through the post. This she handed up to David, who recognised his old friend's writing, which indeed had caught his eye on most of the other envelopes also. And when she had put these back in her pocket she held out her dirty-gloved hand.

"So long," she said. "You won't know me when I turn up on Monday."

"Stop!" cried David. "You must let me know when to send the buggy for you, and where to. It'll never do to have you coming out in the 'bus again."

"Right you are. I'll let you know. So long again—and see here. I think you're the sweetest and trustingest old man in the world!"

She was far ahead, this time, before the buggy was under way again.

"Naturally," chuckled David, following her hair through the crowd. "I should hope so, indeed, when it's a child of John William Oliver, and one that you can love for her own sake an' all! But what made her look so sorry when she gave me the kiss? And what's this? Nay, come, I must have made a mistake!"

He had flattered himself that his eyes never left the portals where they had lost sight of the red hair, and when he got up to it what should it be but the stage door? The words were painted over it as plain as that. The mistake might be Missy's; but a little waiting by the curb convinced Mr. Teesdale that it was his own; for Missy never came back, as he argued she must have done if she really had gone in at the stage door.

CHAPTER V

A WATCH AND A PIPE

Mr. Teesdale drove on to the inn at which he was in the habit of putting up when in town with the buggy. His connection with the house was very characteristic. Many years before the landlord had served him in a menial capacity, but for nearly as many that worthy had been infinitely more prosperous than poor David, who, indeed, had never prospered at all. They were good friends, however, for the farmer had a soul too serene for envy, and a heart too simple to be over-sensitive concerning his own treatment at the hands of others. Thus he never resented his old hand's way with him, which would have cut envy, vanity, or touchiness, to the quick. He came to this inn for the sake of old acquaintance; it never occurred to him to go elsewhere; nor had he ever been short or sharp with his landlord before this evening, when, instead of answering questions and explaining what had brought him into Melbourne twice in one day, Mr. Teesdale flung the reins to the ostler, and himself out of the yard, with the rather forbidding reply that he was there on business. He was, indeed; though the business was the birth of the last half-hour.

It led him first to a little bare office overlooking a yard where many milk-carts stood at ease with their shafts resting upon the ground; and the other party to it was a man for whom Mr. Teesdale was no match.

"I must have twenty pounds," said David, beginning firmly.

"When?" replied the other coolly.

"Now. I shan't go home without it."

"I am very sorry, Mr. Teesdale, but I'm afraid that you'll have to."

"Why should I," cried David, smacking his hand down on the table, "when you owe me a hundred and thirty? Twenty is all I ask, for I know how you are situated; but twenty I must and shall have."

"We simply haven't it in the bank."

"Nay, come, I can't believe that."

"I'll show you the pass-book."

"I won't look at it. No, I shall put the matter into the hands of a solicitor. Good evening to you. I dare say it isn't your fault; but I must have some satisfaction, one way or the other. I am not going on like this a single day longer."

"Good evening, then, Mr. Teesdale. If you do what you say, we shall have to liquidate; and then you will get nothing at all, or very little." David had heard this story before. "It was an evil day for me when I sent you my first load of milk," he cried out bitterly; but in the other's words there had been such a ring of truth as took all the sting out of his own.

"It will be a worse one for us when you send me your last," replied the man of business. "That would be enough to finish us in itself, without your solicitor, in our present state; whereas, if you give us time—"

"I have given you too much time already," said the farmer, heaving the sigh which was ever the end of all his threats; and with a sudden good-humoured resignation (which put his nature in a nutshell), he got up and went away, after an amicable discussion on the exceeding earliness of summer with the man for whom he was no match at all. Throughout his life there had been far too many men who were more than a match for poor David in all such matters.

But the getting of the twenty pounds was a matter apart. He did not want it for himself; the person in need of the money was the child of his dear old friend, who had charged her to apply to him, David, in precisely that kind of difficulty which had already arisen. The fact made the old man's heart hot on one side and cold on the other; for while it glowed with pride at the trust reposed in him, it froze within his breast at the thought of his own helplessness to fulfil that trust. This, however, was a thought which he obstinately refused to entertain. He had not twenty pounds in the bank; on the contrary, his account was overdrawn to the utmost limit. For himself, he would have starved rather than borrow from his friend the innkeeper; but he could have brought himself to do so for Miriam, had he not been perfectly certain that his old servant would refuse to lend. In all Melbourne there was no other to whom he could go for the twenty pounds; yet have it he must, by hook or crook, that night; and ten minutes after his fruitless interview with the middleman who sold his milk, a way was shown him.

He was hanging about the corner of Bourke and Elizabeth Streets, watching the multitude with an absent, lack-lustre eye; the post-office clock had chimed the hour overhead, and David, still absently, had taken his own cherished watch from his waistcoat pocket to check its time. It was not on his last day in Melbourne, nor on his last but one, that the watch had been set by the post-office clock, yet it was still right to the minute; and before the eighth clang from above had been swallowed in the city's hum, David had got his idea. He closed the gold case with a decisive snap, and next moment went in feverish quest of the nearest pawnbroker.

It was with a face strangely drawn between joy and regret, between guilt and triumph, that Mr. Teesdale at length returned to his inn. Here, in the writing-room, now with the scared frown of a forger, and now with a senile giggle, he cowered over a blotting-pad for some minutes; and thereafter returned to the post-office with a sealed envelope, which he shot into safety with his own hands. It was well after nine before the horse was put to, and David seated once more in the buggy, with the collar of his dust-coat turned up about his ears and the apron over his long lean legs.

"Never knew you so late before, old man," said his former servant, who was smoking a cigar in the yard, and perhaps still thinking of his first snub from David Teesdale.

"No, I don't think you ever did," replied David, blandly.

"Second time in to-day, too."

"Second time in," repeated Mr. Teesdale, drawing the reins through his fingers.

"And it'll take you a good hour to get home. I say, you'll be getting into trouble. You won't be there before—What time is it now, old man?"

"Look at the post-office," said David, as he took up his whip.

"I can't see it without going out into the street; besides, I always thought they took their time from that wonderful watch of yours?"

"You're a clever fellow!" cried David, as the other had never heard him speak in the whole course of their previous acquaintance; and he was gone without another word.

He drove away with a troubled face; but the Melbourne street-lamps showed deeper furrows under the old tall hat than David carried with him into the darkness beyond the city, for the more he thought of it, the surer did he become that his late action was not only defensible, but rather praiseworthy into the bargain. There was about it, moreover, a dramatic fitness which charmed him no less because he did not know the name for it. Throughout his unsuccessful manhood he had treasured a watch, which was as absurd in his pocket as a gold-headed cane in a beggarman's hand, because Oliver had given it to him. For years it must have mocked him whenever he took it from his shabby pocket, but in the narrowest straits he had never parted with it, nor had his gold watch ever ceased to be David Teesdale's most precious possession. And now, after two-and-thirty years, he had calmly pawned it, on the spur of the moment, and, as it seemed to himself, for the most extraordinary and beautiful reason in the world; for what he could never bring himself to do in his own need he had done in a moment for the extravagant behoof of his friend's daughter; and his heart beat higher than for many a year in the joy of his deed. So puffed up was he, indeed, that he forgot the fear of Mrs. Teesdale, and some other things besides; for at the foot of the last hill, within a mile of the farm, the horse shied so suddenly that David, taken off his guard, found his near wheels in the ditch before he could haul in the slack of the reins; and when another plunge might have overturned the buggy, a man ran out of the darkness to the horse's head, and before David could realise what had happened his ship had righted itself and was at anchor in the middle of the road.

"My fault, as I'm a sinner!" cried a rich voice from near the horse's ears.

"Nay, I'm very much obliged to you," said Mr. Teesdale, with a laugh, for he made no work of a bit of danger, much less when past.

"But it was me your horse shied at," returned the other, and fell to petting the frightened animal with soft words and a soothing hand. "I was going to take the liberty of stopping you for a moment."

"I never saw you," said David; "it was that dark, and I was that busy thinking. What is it I can do for you? The horse 'll stand steady now, thank you, if you'll come this way."

The wayfarer came round to the buggy wheels and stood still, feeling in all his pockets before answering questions. The near lamp shot its rays upon a broad, deep chest, and showed a pair of hairy hands searching one pocket after another. The rays reached as high as a scarlet neckcloth, but no higher, so that the man's face was not very easily visible; and David was only beginning to pick out of the night a heavy moustache, and a still heavier jaw, when from between the two there came the gleam of teeth, and the fellow was laughing a little and swearing more. He had given up his search, and stood empty-handed under the lamp.

"I'm not a bushranger," said he, "but you might easily think me one."

"Why so?" asked David.

"Because I stopped you to ask for a match to light my pipe, and now I'm hanged if I can find my pipe in any of my pockets; and it was the best one ever I smoked," said the man, with more of his oaths.

"That's a bad job," said David, sympathetically, in spite of a personal horror of bad language, which was one of his better peculiarities.

"A bad job?" cried the man. "It would be that if I'd lost my pipe, but it's a damned sight worse when it's a girl that goes and shakes it from you, and she the biggest little innocent you ever clapped eyes on. Yet she must have shook it. Confound her face!"

He was feeling in his pockets again, but as unsuccessfully as before. The farmer inquired whether he was on his way back to Melbourne, and suggested it was a long walk.

"It is so," said the man; "but it's a gay little town when you get there, is Melbourne—what?"

"Very," said Mr. Teesdale, to be civil; but he was beginning to find this difficult.

"You prefer the country—what?" continued the other, who was now leaning on the wheel, and showing a face which the old man liked even less than the rest of him, it was so handsome and yet so coarse. "Well, so do I, for a change. And talk of the girls!" The fellow winked. "Old Country or Colonies, it's all the same—you give me a country lass for a lark that's worth having. But damn their souls when they lose your favourite pipe!"

"What sort of a pipe was it?" asked David, to change a conversation which he disliked. "If I come across it I'll send it to you, if you tell me where to."

"Good, old man!" cried the stranger. "It was a meerschaum, with a lady's hand holding of the bowl, and coloured better than any pipe ever you saw in your life. If you do find it, you leave it with the boss of the 'Bushman's Rest'. then I'll get it again when next I come this way—to see my girl. For I can't quite think she's the one to have touched it, when all's skid and done."

"Very good," said David, coldly, because both look and word of this roadside acquaintance were equally undesirable in his eyes. "Very good, if I find it. And now, if you'll allow me, I'll push on home."

The other showed himself as ready with a sneer as with an oath. "You are in a desperate hurry!" said he.

"I am," said David; "nevertheless, I'm much obliged to you for being so clever with the horse just now, and I wish you a very good night." And with that, showing for once some little decision, because this kind of man repelled him, old Tees-dale cracked his whip and drove on without more ado.

Nor is it likely he would have thought any more about so trifling an incident, but for another which occurred before he finally reached home. It was at his own slip-rails, not many minutes later; he had got down and taken them out, and was in the act of leading through, when his foot kicked something hard and small, so that it rattled against one of the rails, and shone in the light of the buggy lamp at the same instant. The farmer stopped to pick it up, found it a meerschaum pipe, and pulled a grave face over it for several moments. Then he slipped it into his pocket, and after putting up the rails behind him, was in his own yard in three minutes. Here one of the men took charge of horse and buggy, and the master went round to the front of the house, but must needs stand in the verandah to spy on Arabella, who was sitting with her Family Cherub under the lamp and the blind never drawn. She was not reading; her head was lifted, and she was gazing at the window—at himself, David imagined; but he was wrong, for she never saw him. Her face was flushed, and there was in it a wonder and a stealthy joy, born of the romantic reading under her nose, as the father thought; but he was wrong again; for Arabella had finished one chapter before the coming of Missy, and had sat an hour over the next without taking in a word.

"So you've got back, father?" she was saying presently, in an absent, mechanical sort of voice.

"Here I am," said Mr. Teesdale; "and I left Missy at the theatre, where it appears she had to meet—"

"Missy!" exclaimed Arabella, remembering very suddenly. "Oh yes! Of course. Where do you say you left her, father?"

"At the Bijou Theatre, my dear, I am sorry to say; but it wasn't her fault; it was the friends she is staying with whom she had to meet there. Well, let's hope it won't do her any harm just once in a way. And what have you been doing, my dear, all the evening?"

"I? Oh, after milking I had a bit of a stroll outside."

"A stroll, eh? Then you didn't happen to see a man hanging about our slip-rails, did you?"

Mr. Teesdale was emptying his pockets, with his back to Arabella, so he never knew how his question affected her.

"I wasn't near the slip-rails, I was in the opposite direction," she said presently. "Why do you ask?"

"Because I found this right under them," said Mr. Teesdale, showing her the meerschaum pipe before laying it down on the chimney-piece; "and as I was getting near the township, I met a man who told me he'd lost just such a pipe. And I didn't like him, my dear, so I only hope he's not coming after our Mary Jane, that's all."

Mary Jane was the farm-servant. She had not been out of the kitchen since milking-time, said Arabella; and her father was remarking that he was glad to hear this, when the door flew open, and Mrs. Teesdale whistled into the room like a squall of wind.

"At last!" she cried. "Do you know how long you've been, David? Do you know what time it is?"

"I don't, my dear," said he.

"Then look at your watch."

"My dear," he said, "I've left my watch in Melbourne."

"In Melbourne!" cried Mrs. Teesdale among her top notes. "And what's the meaning of that?"

"It means," said Mr. Teesdale, struggling to avoid the lie direct, "that it hasn't been cleaned for years, and that it needed cleaning very badly indeed."

"But you told Miriam how well it was going; time we were having our teas!"

"Yes, I know, and—that's the curious thing, my dear. It went and stopped on our way in." For there was no avoiding it, after all; yet in all the long years of their married life, it was his first.

CHAPTER VI

THE WAYS OF SOCIETY

The Monday following was the first and the best of some bad days at the farm; for Missy had never written to tell Mr. Teesdale when and where he might call for her, so he could not call at all, and she did not come out by herself. This they now firmly expected her to do, and David wasted much time in meeting every omnibus; but when the last one had come in without Missy, even he was forced to give her up for that day. There would be a letter of explanation in the morning, said David, and shut his ears to his wife's answer. She had been on tenter-hooks all day, for ever diving into the spare room with a duster, dodging out again to inquire what time it was now, and then scolding David because he had not his watch—a circumstance for which that simpleton was reproaching himself before long.

For there was no letter in the morning, and no Missy next day, or the next, or the next after that. It was then that Mr. Teesdale took to lying awake and thinking much of the friendly ticking that had cheered his wakefulness for thirty years, and even more of a few words in the Thursday's Argus, which he had not shown to a soul. And strange ideas concerning the English girl were bandied across the family board; but the strangest of all were John William's, who would not hear a word against her; on the contrary, it was his father, in his opinion, who was to blame for the whole matter, which the son of the house declared to be a mere confusion of one Monday with another.

"You own yourself," said he, "that the girl wanted a new rig-out before she'd come here to stay. Did she say so, father, or did she not? Very well, then. Do you mean to tell me she could get measured, and tried on, and fixed up all round in four days, and two of 'em Saturday and Sunday? Then I tell you that's your mistake, and it wasn't Monday she said, but Monday week, which is next Monday. You mark my words, we'll have her out here next Monday as ever is!"

How John William very nearly hit the mark, and how shamefully Arabella missed it with the big stones she had been throwing all the week—how rest returned to the tortured mind of Mr. Teesdale, and how Mrs. T. was not sorry that she had left the clean good sheets on the spare bed in spite of many a good mind to put them away again—all this is a very short story indeed. For Missy reappeared on the Saturday afternoon while they were all at tea.

Arabella was the one who caught first sight of the red sunshade bobbing up the steep green ascent of the farmhouse, for Arabella sat facing the window; but it was left to John William to turn in his chair and recognise the tall, well-dressed figure at a glance as it breasted the hill.

"Here she is—here's Miriam!" he cried out instantly. "Now what did I tell you all?" He was rolling down his shirt-sleeves as he spoke, flushed with triumph.

Mr. Teesdale had risen and pressed forward to peer through the window, and as he did so the red sunshade waved frantically. Beneath it was a neat straw hat, and an unmistakable red-fringed face nodding violently on top of a frock of vestal whiteness. Arabella flew out to meet the truant, and John William to put on a coat.

"Well, well!" said Mr. Teesdale, holding both her hands when the girl was once more among them. "Well, to be sure; but you're just in time for tea, that's one good thing."

"Nay, I must make some fresh," cried his wife, without a smile. "Mind, I do think you might have written, Miriam. You have led us a pretty dance, I can tell you that." She caught up the teapot and whisked out of the room.

"Have I?" the girl asked meekly of the old man.

"No, no, my dear," and "Not you," the two Teesdales answered in one breath; though the father added, "but you did promise to write."

"I know I did. But you see—"

Missy laughed.

"You should have written, my dear," David said gently, as she got no further, and he had no wish to cross-question her. "I didn't know what had got you."

"None of us could think," added Arabella.

"Except me, Miriam," said John William, proudly. "You were getting your new rig-out; wasn't that it?"

The girl nodded and beamed at him as she said that it was. The sunshade was lying on the sofa now, and Missy sitting at the table in Arabella's place.

"I thought," said Mr. Teesdale, "that you had gone off to Sydney, and weren't coming near us any more. Do you know why? There was a Miss Oliver in the list of the overland passengers in Thurday's Argus."

"Indeed," said the girl.

"Yes, and it was a Miss M. Oliver, and all."

"Well, I never! That's what you'd call a coincident, if you like."

"I'm very glad it was nothing worse," said Mr. Teesdale heartily. "I made that sure it was you."

"You never mentioned it, father?" said John William.

"No, because I was also quite sure that she would write if we only gave her time. You ought to have written, Missy, and then I'd have gone in and fetched you—"

"But that's just what I didn't want. All this way! No, the 'bus was quite good enough for me."

"But what about your trunk?" Arabella inquired.

Missy made answer in the fewest words that her trunk was following by carrier; and because Mrs. Teesdale entered to them now, with a pot of fresh tea, Missy said little more just then, except in specific apology for her remissness in not writing. This apology was made directly to Mrs. Teesdale, whose manner of receiving it may or may not have discouraged the visitor from further conversation at the moment. But so it seemed to one or two, who heard and saw and felt that such discouragement would exist eternally between that old woman and that young girl.

Milking-time was at hand, however, and Missy was left to finish her tea with only Mr. Teesdale to look after her. John William and his mother were the two best milkers on the farm, and Arabella was a fair second to them when she liked, but that was not this evening. Her heart was with Missy in the parlour. But Missy herself was far better suited in having the old farmer all to herself. With him she was entirely at her ease. The moment they were alone she was thanking David for the twenty pounds duly received at the post-office, and his immediate stipulation that the matter of the loan must be a secret made it also an additional bond of sympathy between these two. They sat chatting about England and Miriam's parents, but not more than Missy could help. She referred but lightly to a home-letter newly received, as though there was no news in it; she was much more ready to hear how Mr. Teesdale had had the coat torn off his back in rescuing his first home-letters from the tiny post-office of the early days, which had been swept away by the first wave of the gold-rush. Again he spoke of that golden age, and of his own lost chances, without a perceptible shade of regret, and again Missy marvelled; as did Mr. Teesdale yet again, and in his turn, at her tone about money who had been brought up in the midst of it. It only showed the good sense of his old friend in keeping his children simple and careful amid all their rich surroundings; but Mr. Oliver had been ever the most sensible, as well as the kindest of men. The farmer said this as he was walking slowly in the paddock, with a pipe in his mouth and Missy on his arm, and his downcast eyes upon the long, broken shadow of his own bent figure. Missy's trunk came about this time, but she let it alone. And these two were feeding the chickens together—old David's own department—when Arabella came seeking Missy, having escaped from the milking-stool a good hour before her time.

"Oh, here you are! Come, and I'll help you unpack. Mother said I was to," said she hurriedly. She was only in a hurry for Missy's society. So Missy went with her, getting a good-humoured nod from the old man, whose side she was sorry to leave.

And David watched her out of sight, smiling his calm, kind smile. "She's her father's daughter," said he to the chickens. "Her ways are a bit new to me—but that's where I like 'em. Mannerisms she may have—I wouldn't have her otherwise. She's one of the rising generation—but she has her father's heart, and that's the best kind that ever beat time."

In Missy's bedroom much talking was being done by Arabella. Her curiosity was insatiable, but she herself never gave it a chance. She wanted to know this, but before there was time for an answer she must know that. One thing, when the trunk was unpacked and its contents put away in drawers, she was left entirely unable to understand; and that was, how Missy came to have everything brand-new.

"Why, because everything was spoilt," said Missy, in apparent wonder at the other's wonderment.

"By that one wave?"

"Why, of course."

"But how did it happen?"

"Didn't I tell you? We'd left the window open, and in comes a green sea and half fills the cabin. The captain, he was ever so wild, and, oh my! didn't he give it us! Of course, all our things were spoilt—me and the other girls. We finished the voyage in borrowed everything, and in borrowed everything I came here the other day. Did you think them things were mine? Not much, my dear. Not much! But I was forced to have things of my own before I could come out here and stay."

Arabella, sitting on the bed, studied the tall figure with arms akimbo that struck sharp through the dusk against the square-paned window. She was wondering whether the Olivers were such well-to-do people after all. Her own English was not perfect, but her ear was better than her tongue, and the young ladies in the Family Cherub spoke not at all as Missy spoke. Arabella's next question seemed irrelevant.

"Did you see much society at home, Missy?"

"You bet I did!" was the answer, and the fuzzy head was nodding against the window.

"Real high society, like you read about in tales, Missy?"

"Rather!"

"Lords?"

"Any jolly quantity of lords!"

"You really mean it, Missy?"

"Mean it? What do you mean? Look here, I won't tell you no more if you think I'm telling lies."

"Missy, I never thought of such a thing—never!" Arabella hastened to aver. "I was only surprised, that's all I was.'.isn't likely I meant to doubt your word."

"Didn't you? That's all right, then. Why, bless your heart, do you think it so wonderful to know a few lords?"

"I didn't think they were as common as all that," said Arabella, meekly.

"Common as mud," cried Missy grandly. "Why, you can't swing a cat without knocking a lord's topper off—not in England!"

Arabella laughed. Then her questions ceased for the time being, and Missy was curious to know how she had impressed a rather tiresome interlocutor, for now in the bedroom it was impossible for them to see each other's faces. A few minutes later Missy was satisfied on this point. At the supper-table she had no more attentive listener than Arabella, who watched her in the lamplight as one who has merely read watches another who has seen and done, while Missy rattled on more freely than she had done yet before Mrs. Teesdale. Even Mrs. Teesdale was made to smile this time, though she did her best to conceal it. The visitor was in such racy form.

"I may have to go back home again any day," she told them all. "It'll depend how my mother is, and how they all get on without me. I'll bet they manage pretty badly. But while I am here I mean to make the most of my time. A short life and a merry one, them's my sentiments, ladies and gentlemen! So I want to learn to shoot and milk and do everything but ride. I could ride if I wanted to; I learnt when I was a kid; but a horse once—"

She broke off, laughing and nodding knowingly at Mr. Teesdale, who explained how Missy had been once bitten and was twice shy. John William said that he could very well understand it; and he offered to take Missy out 'possum-shooting as soon as ever there was a moon.

"Have you ever fired a gun, Missy?" said Mr. Teesdale; and Missy shook her head.

"P'r'aps you wouldn't like to try?" said John William.

"Wouldn't I so!" cried the girl, with flashing eyes. "You show me how, and I'll try to-morrow."

"To-morrow's Sunday," Mrs. Teesdale said solemnly. "Is your cup off, Miriam?"

It was not, and because the cocoa was too hot for her Missy poured it into the saucer, and drank until her face was all saucer and red fringe. This impressed Arabella.

"We'll soon teach Missy to shoot," remarked Mr. Teesdale, smiling into his plate, "if she'll hold the gun tight and not mind the noise."

"I'll do my level," said Missy gamely.

John William proceeded to assure her that she could not be taught by a better man than his father, whom he declared to be the best shot in that colony for his age. The old man looked pleased, praise from his son being a very rare treat to him. But Arabella had been neglecting her supper to watch and listen to the guest, and now she asked, "Do the fine ladies shoot in England, Missy?"

"Not they!" replied Missy promptly. "I should like to catch them."

"What ladies do you mean, my dear?" asked the farmer of his daughter.

"Grand ladies—countesses and viscountesses and the rest. Missy knows heaps of them—don't you, Missy?"

"Well, a good few," said Missy, with some show of modesty.

"To be sure you would," murmured Mr. Tees-dale, adding, as his eyes glistened, "and yet you'll come and stay with the likes of us! You aren't too proud to take us as you find us—you aren't above drinking cocoa with your supper."

"What do the lords and ladies drink with their suppers?" asked Arabella, as Missy smiled and blushed.

But the farmer cried, "Their dinners, she means; I'll warrant they dine late every night o' their lives."

Missy nodded to this.

"But what do they drink with their dinners?" repeated Arabella.

"Oh, champagne."

"What else?"

"What else? Oh! claret, and port, and sherry wine. And beer and spirits for them that prefers 'em!"

"All that with their dinners?"

"Rather! I should think they did. The whole lot, one after the other!"

"What! Beer and brandy and sherry wine?" Arabella's incredulity was disagreeably apparent.

"Yes, everything you can think of; but look here, if you don't want to believe me, you needn't, you know!" said Missy, turning as red as her fringe as she stared the other girl full in the eyes across the supper-table. In the awkward pause following John William turned and glared furiously at his sister; but it was their father who cleared the air by saying mildly:

"Arabella, my dear, I'm afraid you don't know a joke when you hear one."

Then Arabella coloured in her turn.

"Do you mean to say you were joking, Missy?" she leant forward to ask; as though she could no more believe this than recent statements.

But Missy had given one quick glance at Mr.

Teesdale, and then, with a little gasp, had burst into an immoderate fit of laughter.

"Of course I was," she cried out as soon as she could speak; "of course I was joking—you old silly!"

CHAPTER VII

MOONLIGHT SPORT

So the first few days were largely spent in teaching Missy to shoot. A very plucky pupil she made, too, if not a particularly apt one; but head and chief of her sporting qualities was her enthusiasm. That was intense. The girl was never happy without a gun in her hand. So far as safety went, she took palpable pains to follow every injunction in the matter of full-cock and half-cock, and laid to heart all the rules given her for the carrying and handling of a loaded firearm. Thus, no one feared her prowling about the farm on tiptoe with John William's double-barrels pointing admirably to earth; least of all, the sparrows and parrots which she never hit. Old Teesdale would go with her and stand chuckling at her side when she missed a sparrow sitting; once he snatched the smoking gun from her, and with the other barrel picked off the same small bird on the wing. Then there was much practice at folded newspapers, of which Missy could sometimes make a sieve, at her own range; and altogether these two shots enjoyed themselves. Certainly it was a sight to see them together—the weak-kneed old man, who could shoot so cleverly still, when he had a mind, and the jaunty young woman who was all slang and fun and rollicking good-nature, plus a cockney lust for blood and feathers.

Missy's first feathers, however, were not such as she might stick in her hat, and her first blood was exceedingly ill-shed. To be sure, she knew no better until the deed was done, and the quaint dead bird with the big head and beak carried home in triumph to Mr. Teesdale. That triumph was short-lived.

"Got one at last!" cried Missy, as she dropped her prey at the old man's feet. Mr. Teesdale was smoking in the verandah, and he pulled a long face behind his smile.

"So I see," said he; "but do you know what it is you have got, Missy?"

"No, I don't, but I mean to have him stuffed, whatever he is."

"I think I wouldn't, Missy, if I were you. It's a laughing jackass."

"Yes? Well, I guess he won't laugh much more!"

"And there's a five-pound penalty for shooting him, Missy. He kills the snakes, therefore you are not allowed by law to kill him. You have broken the law, my dear, and the best thing that we can do is to bury the victim and say nothing about it to anybody." He was laughing, but the girl stood looking at her handiwork with a very red face.

"I thought I was to shoot everything," she said. "I thought that everything eat the fruit and things. I never knew I was so beastly cruel!"

She put away the gun, and spent most of that summer's day in reading to Mr. Teesdale, for whom she had developed a very pretty affection. They read longest in the parlour, with the window shut, and the blind down, and a big fly buzzing between it and the glass. The old man fell sound asleep in the end, whereupon Missy sat very still indeed, just to watch him. And what it was exactly in the worn and white-haired face that fetched the tears to her eyes and the shame to her cheeks, on this particular occasion, there is no saying; but Missy was scarcely Missy during the remainder of the afternoon.

That evening, however, had already been pitched upon for some 'possum-shooting, given a good moon. From the moment she was reminded of this, at tea-time, the visitor was herself again, and something more. It is saying a good deal, but they had not hitherto seen her in such excessively high spirits as overcame her now. She lent Mr. Tees-dale a hand to load some cartridges in the gunroom while the others were milking; but she was rather a hindrance than a help to that patient old man. She would put in the shot before the powder. Then she got into pure infantile mischief, letting off caps under David's coat-tails, and doing her best to make him sharp with her. Herein she failed; nevertheless, the elder was glad enough to hand her over to the younger Teesdale when the time came, and with it a moon without a cloud. Neither Arabella nor her father was going, but three of the men were who worked on the place, and with whom John William was obliged to leave Missy alone in the yard while he went for the dogs. It was only for a minute or two; but the men were in fits of laughter when he returned. It appeared that Missy had been giving them some sort of a dance under that limelit moon.

"Down, Major! Down, Laddie!" John William cried at the dogs as they leaped up at Missy.

But Missy answered, "Down yourself, Jack—I like 'em." And the three men laughed; in fact, they seemed prepared to laugh at Missy whenever she opened her mouth; but John William laughed too as he led the way into the moonlit paddocks.

Here the hunting-ground began without preliminary, for on this side of the farm there were trees and to spare, the land dipping in a gully full of timber before it rose to the high ploughed levels known as the Cultivation. The gully was well grassed for all its trees, which were divers as well as manifold. There were gum-trees blue and red, and stringy-barks, and she-oaks, each and all of them a haunt of the opossum and the native cat. The party promptly surrounded a blue gum at the base of which the dogs stood barking, and Missy found herself doing what the others did—getting the moon behind the branches and searching for what she was told would look more like the stump of a bough or a tangle of leaves than any known animal.

"I believe it's a lie," said John William; "for Laddie barked first, and Laddie always did tell lies."

"Tell lies?" echoed Missy, with a puzzled grin.

"Yes, barking up trees where there's nothing at all—that's what we call telling lies; and old Laddie's started the evening well by telling one already."

"Not he," cried a shrill voice; and the youngest of the three farm-hands—a little bit of a fellow—stood pointing to a branch so low that everyone else had overlooked it.

"I see a little bit of a knot on the bough," said Missy, "but blow me tight if I see anything else!"

"That's it," cried John William. "That little knot is a native cat."

Missy lowered her gun at once. "Oh, I didn't come out," said she, "to shoot cats!"

"But they aren't cats at all," Teesdale explained (while his men stood and laughed); "they're much more like little leopards, I assure you. We only call them cats because—because I'm bothered if I know why! It's not the name for them, as you'll say when you've shot this beggar. And you don't know the way they tear our fowls to pieces, Missy, or you wouldn't make so many bones about it; besides which, you won't get an easier shot all night."

"Oh, if that's the kind of customer, I'm on to try," said Missy. She raised her gun there and then, pressed it to her shoulder, and took aim at the black notch against the silver disc of the moon. The moonlight licked the barrels from sight to sight, getting into Missy's eyes, but there were barely a dozen feet between muzzle and mark. The report was quickly followed by a lifeless thud upon the ground; and when the smoke cleared, that notch was gone from the bough. Then one of the men struck a match to show Missy what she had done; and she had done it so effectually as to give herself a sensation which she concealed with difficulty. It was not pity; there was no pitying a spotted little horror with so sharp a snout and such devilish fangs: but whatever it was, that sensation kept Missy modest in her success, so that she refused the next shot point-blank. John William took it, with the only possible result.

"A bushy." someone said, turning over the dead bush-tailed opossum with his foot It looked very big and soft and gray, lying dead in the moonlight. Missy found it in her heart to pity an opossum.

"Don't you skin them?" she asked at a respectful range. "Do you make no use of them after all?"

"It's so hard not to spoil them," John William said as he slipped another cartridge into the breech. He would have shown her how this particular skin had been ruined by the shot, but Missy said she quite understood.

He was beginning to think her squeamish. He asked her whether she had not had enough. She would not admit it, and took another shot to prove her spirit. This time she failed, and bore her failure with an equanimity which (in Missy) amounted almost to apathy. That she was neither squeamish nor apathetic, however, was demonstrated very suddenly while the night was still young.

A ring-tailed opossum had been brought to earth by a charge from the muzzle-loader of that stunted young colonial whose eyes were as sharp as his voice—he who had "mooned" the native cat. The others called him Geordie. The three of them were kneeling over the dead "ringy," and Missy was taking no more notice of them than she could help; only Geordie's was a voice that made itself heard. Missy had taken little stock of what the kneeling men were doing or saying until suddenly she heard:

"Young'uns it is! I told you there was young 'uns! That little beggar's as dead as his mother, but this one ain't. 'Ere, come off 'er back, can't yer? She ain't no more good to you now, do you 'ear?"

This was Geordie's manner of speech to the bunch of breathing fur that stuck tight to the dead doe's back, whence his fingers were busy disengaging it; but Geordie suddenly found himself on his back in the grass, and when he picked himself up it was Miss Oliver herself who was kneeling where he had knelt, and even going on with his work. It took her some moments, and when done her hands were bloody in the moonshine. Then, first she took that bit of warm fur and nursed it in her neck, stroking it with her chin. And next she turned a calm face up to her companions, and said distinctly to them all, "I call this a damned shame, so I tell you straight!" Indeed she was anything but squeamish.

She lowered her eyes immediately, undid three buttons, and slipped the small opossum into her bosom. There she fixed it, with great care, but not the smallest fuss; and looking up once more, saw the three hirelings walking off together through the trees.

"I tell you," she called after them—shaking her fist at their backs—"I tell you it's the damnedest shame that ever was!"

The words rang clear through the clear night, then found an answer at Missy's side. "You are quite right. It is. And now won't you get up and come back home, Missy?"

"Jack!" cried the girl faintly, as she stumbled to her feet. "I'd quite forgotten you were there."

"I have been here all the time," said John William.

"Then do tell me what I've been saying," said Missy, anxiously, as she took his arm and they started homeward. "I couldn't see no more and keep my scalp fixed. I hope to God I haven't been swearing, have I?"

"Not you, Missy. You've only said what was right and proper. It was cruel, and I blame myself for the whole thing."

"No, no, no! I wanted some sport. I thought I could kill things, and never give a—no, never give a thought to 'em. Now I know I can't. That's all. I say, though, if I did use a swear-word, you won't give me away, will you? I don't know what I said, and that's all about it; but when I lose my scalp—ah well, I know I can trust you."

"Of course you can," said John William cheerily. And involuntarily he pressed to his side the hand that was still within his arm.

"I wouldn't say swear-words unless I did lose my scalp—you understand?" said Missy, coming back to it again.

"Of course you wouldn't; but you didn't."

"I'm not so sure. I wouldn't have your parents hear of it if I did; they'd take it so terribly to heart."

"They shall hear nothing—not that there's anything for them to hear."

"Now my parents are different; they swear themselves."

"Come, I can't credit that, you know!"

"But they do—like troopers!" persisted the girl. "It's the fashion just now in England. You may not know—how should you?"

"Missy," said John William, as he opened her the gate into the homestead yard, "it's impossible to tell when you're joking and when you're not."

"Aha, I mean it to be," cried the girl, bowing low to him, with the moon all over her. Then she stood up to her last inch, smiled full in his face, and turning, left him that smile to keep if he could. He would have followed her, but a burst of laughter in the men's room took him off his course, as good reasons occurred to him for calling in there first.

The room was a part of one of the farm outhouses. In each corner was a bunk, and on each bunk a man (counting Geordie), the fourth being one Old Willie, a retired salt, who drove the milk into Melbourne in the middle of every night. Old Willie was sitting on the side of his bunk and chuckling so windily that the sparks were flying out of his cutty like fireworks. There was nothing, however, to show which of the other three was the entertainer, for each turned silent and looked guilty when John William entered and planted himself in their midst.

"I just thought I'd tell you," said he, with forced blandness, "that there is to be no more 'possum-shooting on this place for good and all. The man who shoots another 'possum, I'll hide him with my own hands, and the man who catches me shooting one, he may take and shoot me. For it's a grand shame, men, it's a grand shame! You heard Miss Oliver say it was, didn't you?" he added sharply, turning to the three.

For the moment they looked blank; the next, it was such a fierce person who was repeating the question, with eyes so like pointed pistols, that one after the other of those three men meekly perjured their souls.

"Exactly," said John William, nodding his head in a deadly calm. "She said it was the grandest shame ever was; and if any man says she said anything else—well, he'd better let me hear him, that's all!"

CHAPTER VIII

THE SAVING OF ARABELLA

One night early in December, Arabella burst into Missy's room with singular abruptness. Missy had said good-night to the others and was very nearly in bed, but she had not seen Arabella, who had been out all the evening. Evidently she had only now come in. She was breathing quickly from hurrying up-hill; and there was a light in her countenance which Missy noticed in due course.

"Missy," she began, as abruptly as she had entered, "do you remember the day you first came, and we showed you that group of you all taken when you were quite little?"

Missy nodded in the looking-glass. She was busy with her fringe.

"Well," continued Arabella, "you said red came out light, talking of your hair. Do you remember that?"

"Red came out light? No, I can't say I do."

"You must, Missy! You were speaking of your hair in that group——"

Missy flourished a brave bare arm. "Now I see. My poor old carrots! Of course they came out light; they couldn't come out red, could they?"

"No; but I'm told that red comes out black—that's all."

Missy faced about in a twinkling. Her bare arms went akimbo. She was pale.

"So that's what excited you, eh?" she cried derisively; yet it was only in the moment of speaking that she perceived that Arabella was excited at all.

"I'm not excited, Missy!"

"No?"

"Not a bit," said Arabella, as she gave herself the scarlet lie from neck to forehead. This amused Missy.

"Then what is it?" said she at last, with a provoking smile which the other could not meet. "Is it only that you're just dying to bowl me out? All right, my dear, we'll put it down to that. Only take care I don't bowl you out too—take very good care that I don't find out something about you!"

Arabella had the pale face now.

"Take very extra special good care," continued Missy, nodding nastily, "that I haven't found out something already!"

"Have you?"

The hoarse voice was unknown to Missy, and the frightened face seemed a fresh face altogether. She read it in a moment, and was laughing the next.

"Of course I haven't, my good girl!"

"O Missy!"

"Just as if you'd done anything you'd mind being found out! No, my dear, I was only having a lark with you; but you deserved it for having one with me. Now as to my hair in that photograph—"

"Oh, but of course I believe you, Missy, and not—and not the person who told me different."

"Now I wonder who that was?" said Missy to herself; but aloud—"That's a blessing! And now if you'll let me go to bed, my dear, we'll neither of us think any more of all this tommy-rot that we've been talking."

Nevertheless she herself thought about it half that night. And a variety of vague suspicions crystallised at last into a single definite conclusion.

"She has a man on," muttered Missy to her pillow. "That's what's the matter with Arabella."

Her mind was fully made up before she slept.

"I must find out something about it; what I do see I don't like; and I've just got to take care of Arabella."

Forthwith she set herself to watch. It was first of all necessary to become really intimate with Arabella. The latter's addiction to personal catechism, to name one thing, had kept Missy not a little aloof hitherto. Now, however, in the nick of time, this weakness passed away, and with it this barrier. There were no more questions asked obviously for the sake of doubting or discrediting the answer. On the other hand, about some things Arabella was as inquisitive as ever; especially to wit, Missy's love affairs. Curiously enough, this was the one point on which Missy was markedly reticent, for very good reasons of her own; but she had no objection to discussing with Arabella the general subject of love. She noted the fascination this had for her companion. When the latter came to speak of her male ideal, from the point of view of his appearance, Missy noted much more. "He has a black moustache and very dark eyes," said she to herself. "That's the kind I trust least of all!" She knew something about it, evidently.

A tiny incident, however, which happened when Missy had been some five or six weeks at the farm, told her more than Arabella had done, directly or indirectly, in any of their conversations. The girls were in the room with Mr. Teesdale, who was looking on the chimney-piece for a lost letter, when he exclaimed suddenly:

"What's got that meerschaum pipe, Arabella?"

"Which one was that, father?" was the only answer, in a suspiciously innocent voice.

"The one I picked up by our slip-rails the night I took Missy back to Melbourne. It belonged to yon man I told you I met on the road. I was saving it in case I ever set eyes on him again."

"Oh, that one!" cried Arabella; then, after a pause, she added, with a nonchalance which Missy for one admired: "I gave it back to him the other day."

"To whom?"

"Why, the man that lost it!"

"You gave it back—to the man that lost it?" cried David, in the greatest surprise, while Missy became buried in the Argus of that morning. "Dear me, where have you seen him, honey?"

"In the township."

"In the township, eh? Now what sort of a man was it that you saw in the township? Tell me what he was like."

"Like? Oh, he had—let's see—he had very dark eyes; oh, yes, and a dark moustache and all; and he was very—well, rather handsome, I thought him."

"Ay, that's near enough," said Mr. Teesdale, greatly puzzled; "quite near enough to satisfy me that he's the same man; but how in the world did you know that he was? That's what I can't make out!"

"Why, he told me himself, to be sure!"

"Ay, but how came he to speak to you at all? That's what I want to know."

"Then I'm sure I can't tell you," said Arabella, with a toss of her head, not badly done. "I suppose he saw where I came from, and I dare say he'd been leaning again' our slip-rails that night he lost his pipe. Anyhow, he asked me whether I'd found one, and I said you had, and he described the one he'd lost, and I knew that must be it. So I came back and got it for him. That was all."

Mr. Teesdale seemed just a little put out. "I wonder you didn't say anything about it at the time, my dear," said he, in mild remonstrance.

"Me? Why, I never thought any more of it," the young woman said, with a slightly superfluous laugh. "I—you see that was the first and last I'd seen of him," added Arabella, as if to end the discussion; but her father had not finished his say.

"I'm glad it was the last, however—I am glad of that!" he exclaimed with unusual energy. "Why? Because, my dear, little as I saw of him, I didn't like the cut of that man's jib. No," said Mr. Teesdale, letting his eyes travel through the window to the river-timber, and shaking his head decidedly, as he sat down in his accustomed seat; "no, I didn't like it at all; and very sorry I should have been to think a man of that stamp was coming here after our Mary Jane!"

And Missy said never a word; but neither word, look nor tone had escaped her.

Her eyes were very wide open now. Arabella went out more evenings than one, but never, it appeared, on two consecutive evenings; so the man was not living in the district. And Missy said so much the worse; he was not merely passing his time. To clinch matters, the unhappy girl began to hang out signs of sleepless nights and perpetual nervous preoccupation by day; signs which Missy alone interpreted aright.

At length, a little before Christmas, there came a night when Arabella kissed them all round and went off to her room much earlier than usual. And the fever in her eyes and lips was noted by Missy, and by Missy alone.

It was a night of stars only. The moon by which Missy had killed her one native cat, and nursed an infant opossum, had waxed and waned. The night, when Mr. Teesdale took a breath of it last thing, looked black as soot. Twenty minutes later, the farmhouse was in utter darkness; not a single ray from a single window; and so it remained for nearly two hours.

Then suddenly a light shone in the parlour for a single instant only. The outer door of the little gun-room was now opened, as noiselessly as might be, and shut again, hairbreadth by hairbreadth. The odd thing was, that this happened not once, but twice within five minutes. And each time it was a woman's figure that stood up under the stars, and then stole forth into the night.

There were two of them; and while the first went swiftly in a given direction (towards the timbered gully), the second made a quick circuit of the premises, and, as it happened, intercepted the first among the trees as though she had been lying in wait there for hours. Then it was "O Missy!" and Arabella uttered a stifled, terrified scream.

"Yes, it's Missy," said that young woman soberly. "And I wonder what we're doing out here at this time of night, both of us?"

"I'm having a walk," said Arabella, giggling half hysterically.

"That's exactly what I'm doing; so we can walk together."

"You've followed me out, you mean liar!" cried Arabella, with wholly hysterical wrath. She had, indeed, been for pushing forward after the first shock, but when Missy stepped out alongside there was nothing for it but a pitched battle on the spot.

"I have so," said Missy. "I know all about it, you see."

"All about what?"

"What you are after."

"And what am I after, since you're so mighty clever?"

"You're meeting that man."

"What man?" Arabella was quaking pitifully. "The man you're always meeting; but to-night you meant to run away with him."

"Spy!" said Arabella. "What makes you think that?"

"You have put on all your best things."

"But what makes you think there is a man at all?"

"Oh, I saw that ages ago; though mind you, I have never seen him. It is the man with the meerschaum pipe, now isn't it?"

Arabella's first answer was a shaking fist. Next moment she was shaking all over, in a storm of tears during which Missy took hold of her with both arms, was thrown off, took a fresh hold, and was then suffered to keep it. At last she asked:

"Where were you to meet him, Arabella?"

The answer came with more sobs than words. "At the top corner of the Cultivation: the road corner: he is to wait there till I come."

"Good!" said Missy. "That's half a mile away, and where we are is out of hearing of the house. Not so sure, eh? Well, come a little, further down the gully. That's better! Now we're safe as the bank, and you'll stop and tell me something about him, won't you, dear, before you go?"

Before she went! Could she ever go now? All the strength which this poor creature had imbibed from a man as masterful as the woman was weak—an imitative courage, never for a moment her honest own—had been rooted up easily enough from the soul where there was no soil for it, and was now as though it had never existed. Such nerve as she had summoned up was gone. Yes, she would stop and talk; that would be a relief. And Missy should hear all, all there was to tell; but this was very little, incredibly little indeed.

On that first evening, when Missy had come and gone, Arabella had taken a stroll by herself after supper; had been thinking more about the Family Cherub story, in which she was then engrossed, than of anything else that she could now remember; but it appeared her head had been full at the time of romantic stuff of one kind or another, so that when she came very suddenly upon a handsome stranger leaning over the slip-rails and smoking his pipe, it was readily revealed to Arabella that she had been waiting for that moment and that stranger all her life. She said as much now, in other words, but wasted time in unnecessary dilatation upon the man's good looks before proceeding with her confession. He had spoken soft words to her in the soft night air. He had kissed her across the slip-rails. And Arabella had lived thirty years in her tiny corner of the world, but never before had she been kissed by the mouth of man not a Teesdale. Missy might stare as much as she liked; it was the sacred truth, was that.

So much for the first meeting, which was a pure accident. There had been others which were nothing of the kind. Missy nodded, as much as to say she knew all about those other meetings, and hurried Arabella to the point. That the foolish girl knew less than nothing worth knowing about this man was only too evident; but it seemed his name was Stanborough. And to-morrow, said Arabella, with a sudden hauling at the slack of her nerves, this would be her name too.

Then she still meant to go?

Arabella fell to pieces again. She had promised. He was waiting. He would kill her if she broke her promise.

"Kill your grandmother!" said Missy. "Let him wait. Shall I tell you who'll kill who if you do go?"

"Who?" said Arabella in a whisper.

"Why, you'll kill your father, as sure as ever God made you, my girl."

"But we should soon come back—and with money enough to help them here tremendously! He has promised that; and you don't know how well off he is, Missy. Yes, yes, we should soon come back after we were married!"

"I dare say—after that," said Missy dryly.

"Then you don't think he—means—"

"Of course he doesn't."

"How do you know?"

"Never mind how I know. It's enough that I do know, as sure as I'm standing under this tree. You've told me quite sufficient. I feel as if I knew your man as well as I've known two or three. The brutes! And I tell you,'.ella, that if you go to him now, as you thought of doing, your life will be blasted from this night on. He will never marry you. He hasn't gone the right way about that. No, but he'll ruin you and leave you in your ruin; and when he does, may the Lord have mercy on your soul!"

She had said. And the extraordinary emotion which had gathered in her voice as she went on had the effect of taking Arabella out of herself even then.

"Missy," she whispered—"Missy, you are crying! How can you know so much that is terrible? You seem to know all about it, Missy!"

"Never mind how much I know, or how I came to know it," cried the other. "I know enough to want to save you from what some girls I've known have come to. To say nothing of saving your dear old father's life. For kill him it would."

Arabella had been marvelling; but now her own difficulty clutched her afresh.

"He will kill me if I don't go to him. He has said so," she moaned in her misery, "and he will."

"Not he! He's a coward. I feel as if I knew the beast—and precious soon I shall."

Arabella started. "What do you mean?" said she.

"I mean that you've got to leave your friend to me. I'll soon settle him."

Missy spoke cheerily. Her new tone inspired confidence in the breast of Arabella, who whispered eagerly, "How can you? Ah, if you only could!"

"You would like it?"

"I should thank God! O Missy, I have been such a wicked, foolish girl, but you are so strong and brave! I shall love you for this all my life!"

"Will you? I wonder," said Missy. "But never mind that now. Go you back to the house, and if I don't come to your room in less than half an hour and tell you that I've sent Mr. Stanborough about his business—"

"Hush!" exclaimed the other in low alarm. "I hear him now. He is coming to look for me."

It was a very faint sound, but terror had sharpened the girl's ears. It was the sound of a walking-stick swishing the dry grass on the further slope of the gully. Missy heard it also when she bent her ear to listen, and the next moment she had her companion by the shoulders.

"Now run." said she, "and run for your life. No, we've no time for any of that stuff now. Time enough to thank me when I come and tell you I've sent him to the right-about for good and all. Run quickly—keep behind the trees—and all will be well before you're an hour older."

And so they separated, Arabella hurrying upward to the farm, her heart drumming against her ribs, while Missy trudged down the hill at her full height, with a marble mouth, and both fists clenched.

CHAPTER IX

FACE TO FACE

For whatever else this wild girl may have been, she was obviously not a coward. That is the one thing to be said for Missy without any hesitation whatever. Alone, and in the night, she was going to pit herself against an unknown man, who was certainly a villain; yet on she went, with her chin in the air and her arms swinging free. The trees were thickest at the bottom of the low gully. The girl came through them with a brisk glance right and left, but never a lagging step. On the further slope the trees spread out again, and here, on comparatively open ground, she did stop, and suddenly. She could smell the man's pipe in the sweet night air; the man himself was nowhere to be seen.

Missy filled her lungs slowly through her teeth, and emptied them with dilated nostrils. Then she went on, longing in her heart for a moon. In the starlight it was not possible to see clearly very many yards ahead. So far as she could see—and her eyes were good—there was no one in that paddock but herself. Yet a faint smell of tobacco still slightly fouled the air. And this was the very worst part of the whole business; it had brought Missy at last to a second stand-still, and to the determination of singing out, when, without warning sound, an arm was flung round her neck, soft words were being whispered in her ear, and Missy who was no coward felt the veins freezing in her body.

She flung herself free with a great effort, then reeled against the she-oak from behind which he had crept who now stood taking off his hat to her in the starlight.

"I beg your pardon," said a rich, suave voice in its suavest tones; "upon my word, I beg your pardon from the very bottom of my heart! I thought—I give you my word I thought you were another young lady altogether!"

Missy had recovered a measure of her customary self-control. "So I see—so I see," she managed to say distinctly enough; but her voice was the voice of another person.

"Thank you, indeed! You are very generous," said the man, raising his hat once more; "few women would have understood. The fact is, as I say, I took you for a certain young lady whom I quite expected to meet before this. Perhaps you have seen her, and could tell me where she is? For we have missed each other among these accursed gum-trees."

The fellow's impudence was good for Missy.

"Yes, I have seen her," said she, as calmly as the other.

"And where may she be at this moment?"

"In her father's house."

The man stood twirling his moustache and showing the white teeth under it. Then he stuck in his mouth a meerschaum he had in his hand, and sucked silently at the pipe for some moments. "I beg your pardon once more; but I fear we are at cross-purposes," said he presently. He had been considering.

"I don't think it," said Missy.

"And why not?" This with a smile.

"Because I have a message for you, Mr. Stan-borough."

"Ha!"

"A message from Arabella Teesdale," said Missy, who had lowered her tone and drawn the other a pace nearer in his eagerness.

"And?" he asked; but he was made to wait. "Will you have the goodness to give me that message? Tell me what she says, can't you?"

"Oh, certainly!" replied Missy, with a laugh. "I was to say that she had been very foolish, but has come to her senses in time; and that you will never see her any more, as she has thought better of it, and is done with you for good and all!"

There was a pause first, and then a short sardonic laugh.

"So you were to say all that! It isn't the easiest thing in the world to take it in all at once. Do you mind saying some of it over again?"

"Once is enough. You've got your warning; it's no good your coming after 'Bella Teesdale no more. If you do, you look out for her brother, that's all!"

"John William, eh?" The man laughed again.

"Yes."

"I know all about the family, you see. I know all about you too—in a way. I never knew you were 'Bella's keeper, I must admit. She merely told me you were a young English lady, of the name of Miss Miriam Oliver, who landed the other week in the Parramatta."

"So I am," said Missy, trembling violently. Her back was still to the good she-oak, but the man had come so close to her now that she could not have escaped him if she would.

"Now that's very interesting," he hissed, so that the moisture from his mouth struck her in the face. "If I'd been asked who you were, d'ye see, without first being told, d'ye know what I should have said? I should have said that the other week—just about the time the Parramatta came in—there was a certain member of the Bijou Chorus, who answered to the name of Ada Lefroy. And I should have said that Miss Miriam Oliver, of England, was so exactly the dead-spit of Miss Ada Lefroy, of the Bijou Theatre, Melbourne, Victoria, Australia, in the Southern Hemisphere, that they must be one and the same young lady. As it is, I'll strike a light and see." He struck one on the spot. Missy was staring at him with still eyes in a white face. He laughed softly, and used the match to relight his meerschaum pipe, which had gone out.

"Well, if this doesn't lick creation!" he murmured, nodding his head very slowly, to look the girl up and down. "To think that I should have missed you from the town and found you in the country! The swell young lady from Home! Good Lord, it's too rich to be true."

Missy opened her lips that had been fast, and under that she-oak her language would have surprised the Teesdales.

"Come, this is more like," said the other clapping his hands in mock approval. "Now you'll feel better, eh? And now you'll tell me how you worked it, I'm sure."

Missy said what she would do instead.

"Then I must just tell myself. Let's see now: your father—ha! ha!—was old Teesdale's old friend, and luckily for you he'd warned them his daughter was something out of the common. That was luck! And you were out of the common! Hasn't 'Bella told me the things you said and did, till I was sick and tired? Faith, I'd have listened better if I'd dreamt it was you! I remember her saying you brought a letter of introduction, however; and that you must have stole, my beauty!"

Missy cleared her throat. "You're a liar," she said. "I found it."

"You found it! That's a lot better, isn't it? A fat lot! Anyhow, out you came, to pose as my young lady from Home till further orders. And my oath, it was one of the cheekiest games I've heard of yet!"

"I only came out for a lark," Missy said sullenly. "It was they that put it into my head to come back and stay. I couldn't help it. It was better here than in Melbourne. Much better!"

"Morally, eh?"

"What do you mean?"

"I mean, this is a cleaner life than t'other—what?"

"It is. Thank God!"

Stanborough laughed. (Missy had known him under another name, but she was hardly in a position to gain anything by reminding him of that.) "A mighty fine life," said he, "with a mighty fine lie at the bottom of it!"

"Yes," said Missy slowly, "that's true enough. But I'm a better sort than when I came here, I know that!"

"A better sort, eh? Ha! ha! ha! That's good, that is. That's very good indeed."

But the girl was too much in earnest to heed the sneers. "You may laugh as you like—it's God's truth," cried she. "And Melbourne will never see me no more, nor London neither. Why? 'Cause when I clear out of this, I clear up-country; and up-country I shall live ever after; yes, and very likely marry and die respectable. So you can go on jeering—"

"Stop! Not so fast," said Stanborough. "You seem to have got it all cut and dried; but when did you think of clearing out of this? Suppose you're safe till there's been time for the mails home and out again. That takes three months; you've been here more than one already, and you meant to stop just one month more. Good! very good indeed. Sorry your one month more has gone so quickly—sorry it's only one more night instead. However, that's the misfortune of war. Quite understand? Not another month— another night only—that's to-night—and a little bit of tomorrow."

Missy remarked at length:

"So you mean to give me away; I might have known that."

"Of course I do. Six months hard, that's what you will get." Missy shuddered. Her tormentor watched her and continued: "So that makes you sit up, does it, my dear? She didn't know she was breaking the law, didn't she? She'll find out soon enough—find out what it costs to pass yourself off as another person, in this Colony—find out what the inside of Carlton Jail's like, too! Not go back to town. That was good, that was."

The girl could only pant and glare and wring her hands. More followed in the same strain.

"Nice night, ain't it? Nice breeze coming up to kiss the leaves and make 'em cry! Hark at 'em, tree after tree. There goes this she-oak over our heads! Nice and cool on your face, too, isn't it? Nice wholesome smell of eucalyptus—and all the rest of it. Oh, a sweet night altogether, and one to remember—for your last night out o' prison!"

"You brute!" said Missy, and worse.

He listened patiently, nodding his head at each name. And then—

"All that? Not so fast, my dear, not half so fast, if you please. You're in far too much of a hurry, I do assure you. All that's supposing I do give you away." The man's tone was changed. "But you're going to."

"No," replied Stanborough, "not if you'll clear right out to-night. Do that and I won't say a word to a soul; not even at the farm will I give you away, once you're gone. It'll just be a case of your going as mysteriously as you came; and they may never find out the truth about you; but even if they do, you'll be far enough before they do. Only clear out to-night!"

"And leave 'Bella to you? I'll see you in blazes—"

"And yourself in quod—"

"I don't care; you're not going to ruin Arabella."

"What if you're too late to prevent it?"

"If I was, you wouldn't be here to-night. You see I know you, too."

There was a pause.

"Do you know what I've half a mind to do?" Stanborough said at length in an exceedingly calm voice.

"Yes; to kill me. But you haven't half the pluck—not you! I know you of old."

"All right, we shall see. I give you the rest of this night to clear out in. If you don't, you may lose me my game; but you may bet your soul, Ada Lefroy, I'll have you locked up before you're a day older."

He shook his fist in her face and went away very abruptly; but in a minute he was back, all eagerness and soft persuasion.

"I have nothing against you, Ada," he began now. "You and I have had fun together. And after all, what have I to gain by getting you locked up? What is it to me if you hoodwink these old people and run your own risk? Why should I want you to clear out to-night? See here, my girl, I don't want you to do anything of the kind. You sit tight as long as you think you can; only go back now, like a sensible sort, and get 'Bella to come along with me, like another."

"I can't."

"You could. It was you who persuaded her not to come. I know it was; so don't tell me you couldn't persuade her that I am all right, and to keep her word with me after all."

"Then I won't say I couldn't I'll say I never will."

"And you mean that?"

"Of course I mean it."

"Well knowing that I shall come and expose you to-morrow, or the next day, or the day after that? By God, it'd be sport to keep you waiting!"

"Then have your sport. Have it! I will never leave 'Bella, that's one thing sure."

"You'd go to prison for her?"

"I'd do anything for any of them."

"Then go to hell for them!"

With that he lifted his clenched fist and struck at the girl's face, but she put up her hands, and only her lip was grazed. When she lowered her hands the man was gone.

And this time he was gone altogether. Missy waited, cowering behind the tree, now on this side, now on that. But there were no more footsteps in the short, dry grass until Missy herself stole out from under that she-oak, and crept down into the gully, with giving knees and her chin on her breast, a very different figure from the bold adventuress who had marched up that same slope a short hour earlier in the night. And the stars were still shining all over the little weather-board homestead, so softly, so peacefully, when Missy got back to it. And in the verandah was the wooden chair in which she would sit to read to Mr. Teesdale, and the wooden chair in which Mr. Teesdale would sit and listen. And Missy glided up and took away their book, which lay forgotten on one of the chairs; and then she glided back, thinking chiefly of the last chapter they had read together. They were hardly likely to read another now. But that was not a nice thought; and the farmhouse lay so still and serene under the stars, it was good to watch it longer; for the little homestead had never before seemed half so sweet or so desirable in the girl's eyes. And these were the only waking eyes just then on the premises, for even Arabella had fallen into a fitful, feverish sleep, from which, however, she was presently awakened in the following manner.

Something hot and dry had touched her hand that was lying out over the coverlet. Something else that was also hot, but not dry, had fallen upon that hand, and more of the same sort were still falling. So Arabella awoke frightened; and there was Missy, kneeling at her bedside, fondling her hand, and sobbing as she prayed aloud. Arabella heard without listening. Days afterwards she took out of her ears two phrases: "whatever I have been" and "bad as I am". These words she put in due season through the mills of her mind; but at the time she simply said:

"Missy! What are you doing? Ah, I remember. Have you seen him? Tell me what he said—what has happened—and what is going to happen now."

"I've seen him and settled him," Missy whispered firmly as she dried her eyes. "What he said isn't of any account. But nothing's going to happen—nothing—nothing at all."

CHAPTER X

THE THINNING OF THE ICE

Old Teesdale sat with his arm-chair drawn close to the table, and his shirt-sleeves rolled up to the elbow. He was writing a letter in which he had already remarked that it was the hottest Christmas Eve within even his experience of that colony. In the verandah, indeed, the thermometer had made the shade heat upwards of 1000 since nine o'clock in the morning, touching 1100 in the early afternoon. It was now about six (Mr. Teesdale being still without his watch was never positive of the time), and because of Mrs. T.'. theory that to open a window was to let in the heat, to say nothing of the flies, the atmosphere of the parlour with its reminiscences of the day's meals was sufficiently unendurable. A little smoke from Mr. Teesdale's pipe would surely have improved it if anything; but that was against the rules of the house, and the poor gentleman, who was not master of it, wrote on and on with the perspiration standing on his bald head, and the reek of the recent tea in his nose.

He was on the third leaf of a letter for the English mail. "As to Miriam herself"—thus the paragraph began which was still being penned—"I can only say that she is the life and soul of our quiet home, and what we shall do without her when she goes I really do not like to think. Referring again to the letter in which you advised me of her arrival, and to those 'habits and ways' of which you warned me, I cannot deny that I soon saw what you meant; but I must say that I would not have Miriam without her 'mannerisms' even if I could. They may be modern, but they are very entertaining indeed to us, who are so far behind the times. Yes, the young girls of our day may have talked less 'slang' and paid more attention to 'appearances,' but no girl ever had a warmer heart than your Miriam, nor a kinder nature, nor a franker way with her in all her dealings. But her kindness is what has struck me most, from the very first, and especially her kindness to an old man like me. You should see her sit and read to me by the hour, and help me with whatever little thing I may happen to be doing, and listen to my talk as though I were a young man like our John William. Then I think you would understand why I am always saying that she never could have been anybody's daughter but yours, and why I want to keep her as long as ever you will let her stay. She has spoken of going on to other friends after the New Year; but I wish you would insist upon her coming back to us for a real long visit before she leaves the colony for good; and I know that you would do so if you could but see the change which even a few weeks with us has already wrought in her. You must know, my dear Oliver, that we live here very simply indeed; but I am of opinion that simple living and early hours were what Miriam needed more than anything else, for it is no exaggeration to say that she does not look the same girl who first came to see us with your letter of introduction. She has a better colour, her whole face is brighter and healthier, and the tired look I at first noticed in her eyes has gone out of them once and—"

At this point Mr. Teesdale paused, pen in air.

He was a very careful letter-writer, who wrote a beautiful old-fashioned hand, and made provision for perfectly even spaces by means of a black-lined sheet nicely adjusted under the leaf; and he rounded each sentence in his own mind before neatly committing it to paper. Thus a single erasure was a great rarity in his letters, while two would have made him entirely rewrite. On the other hand, many a minute here and there were spent in peering through the gun-room window, and scouring the Dandinong Ranges for the right word; and now several minutes went thus in one lump, because Mr. Teesdale was by nature an even greater stickler for the literal truth than for flawless penmanship, and he had caught himself in the act of writing what was not strictly true. It was a fact that the tired look had gone out of Missy's eyes, but to add "once and for all" was to make the whole statement a lie, according to Mr. Teesdale's standard. For the last thirty-six hours that tired look had been back in those bright eyes, which brightened now but by fits and starts. David did not so define it, but the girl looked hunted. He merely knew that she did not look to-day or yesterday as she had looked for some weeks without a break, therefore he could not and would not say that she did. Accordingly the predicate of the unfinished sentence was radically altered until that sentence stood... "and the tired look I at first noticed in her eyes is to be seen in them but very seldom now."

But the erasure had occurred on the fifth page, on a new sheet altogether, which it was certainly worth while to commence afresh; and old Tees-dale had scarcely regained the point at which he had tripped when the door opened, and the subject of his letter was herself in the room beside him, looking swiftly about her, as if to make certain that he was alone, before allowing her eyes to settle upon his welcoming smile.

"Well, Missy, and what have you been doing with yourself since tea?"

"I?" said the girl absently, as she glanced into the gun-room, and then out of each window, very keenly, before sitting down on the sofa. "I? Oh, I've been having a sleep, that's what I've been doing."

Mr. Teesdale was watching her narrowly as he leant back in his chair. She did not look to him as though she had been sleeping; but that was of course his own fancy. On the other hand, the strange expression in Missy's eyes, which he could not quite define, struck the old man as stranger and more conspicuous than ever.

"I'm afraid, my dear, that you haven't been getting your proper sleep lately."

"You're right. There's no peace for the wicked these red-hot nights, let alone the extra wicked, like me."

"Get away with you!" said old Teesdale, laughing at the grave girl who was staring him in the face without the glimmer of a smile.

"Get away I will, one of these days; and glad enough you'll be when that day comes and you know all about me. I've always told you a day like that would come sooner or later. It might come to-morrow—it might come to-night!"

"Missy, my dear, I do wish you'd smile and show me you're only joking. Not that it's one of your best jokes, my dear, nor one of your newest either. Ah, that's it—that's better!"

She had jumped up to look once more out of the window: a man was passing towards the hen-yard, it was little Geordie, and Missy sat down smiling.

"Then tell me what it is you're busy with," she began in a different tone; an attempt at the old saucy manner which the farmer loved as a special, sacred perquisite of his own.

"Now you're yourself again! I'm writing a long, long letter, Missy. Guess who to?"

"To—to Mr. Oliver?"

"Mr. Oliver! Your father, my dear—your own father! Now guess what it's about, if you can!"

"About—me?"

David nodded his head with great humour.

"Yes, it's about you. A nice character I'm giving you, you may depend!"

"Are you saying that I'm a regular bad lot then?"

"Ah, that's telling!"

"If you were, you wouldn't be far from the mark, if you only knew it. But let's hear what you have said."

"Nay, come! You don't expect me to let you hear what I've said about you, do you, Missy?"

"Of course I do," said Missy firmly.

"But that would be queer! Nay, Missy, I couldn't show you this letter, I really couldn't. For one thing, it would either make you conceited or else very indignant with poor me!"

"So that's the kind of character you've been giving me, is it?" said Missy, smiling grimly. "Now I must see it."

"Nay, come, I don't think you must, Missy—I don't think you must!"

"But I want to."

So exclaiming, the girl rose resolutely to her feet; and her resolution settled the matter; for it will have been seen that the weak old man himself was all the time wishing her to see what he had written about her. After all, why should she not know how fond he was of her? If it made her ever such a little bit fonder of him, well, there surely could be no harm in that. Still, Mr. Tees-dale chose to walk up and down the room while Missy stood at the window to read his letter, for it was now growing dark.

"I see you mention that twenty pounds." Missy had looked up suddenly from the letter. "How was it you managed to get the money that night, after all? I have often meant to ask you."

Mr. Teesdale stopped in his walk. "What does it matter how I got them, honey? I neither begged, borrowed nor stole 'em, if that's what you want to know." The old gentleman laughed.

"I want to know lots more than that, because it matters a very great deal, when I went and put you to all that inconvenience."

"Well, I went to the man who buys all our milk. I told you I was going to him, didn't I?"

"Yes, but I've heard you say here at table that you haven't had a farthing from him these six months."

"Missy, my dear," remonstrated the old man, with difficulty smiling, "you will force me to ask you—to mind—"

"My own business? Right you are. What's the time?"

"The time!" The question did indeed seem irrelevant. "I'm sure I don't know, but I'll go and have a look at the kitchen—"

"Then you needn't. I don't really want to know. I was only wondering when John William would be back from Melbourne. But where's your watch?"

"Getting put to rights, my dear," said old Tees-dale faintly, with his eyes upon the carpet.

"What, still?"

"Yes; they're keeping it a long time, aren't they?"

"They are so," said Missy dryly. She watched the old man as he crossed the room twice, with his weak-kneed steps, his white hands joined behind him and his thin body bent forward. Then she went on reading his letter.

It affected her curiously. At the third page she uttered a quick exclamation; at the fourth she lowered the letter with a quick gesture, and stood staring at David with an expression at which he could only guess, because the back of her head was against the glass.

"This is too much," cried Missy in a broken voice. "I can never let you send this."

"And why not, my dear?" laughed Mr. Teesdale, echoing, as he thought, her merriment; for it was to this he actually attributed the break in her voice.

"Because there isn't a word of truth in it; because I haven't a warm heart nor a kind nature, and because I'm not frank in my dealings. Frank, indeed! If you knew what I really was, you wouldn't say that in a hurry!"

Mr. Teesdale could no longer suppose that the girl was in fun. Her bosom was heaving with excitement; he could see that, if he could not see her face. He said wearily:

"There you go again, Missy! I can't understand why you keep saying such silly things."

"I'm not what you think me. You understand that, don't you?"

"I hear what you say, but I don't believe a word of it."

"Then you must! You shall! I can't bear to deceive you a moment longer—I simply can't bear it when you speak and think of me like this. First of all, then, this letter's no good at all!"

In another instant that letter fluttered upon the floor in many pieces.

"You must forgive me," said Missy, "I couldn't help it; it wasn't worth the paper it was written on; and now I'm going to tell you why."

Old Teesdale, however, had never spoken, and this silenced the girl also, for the moment. But that moment meant a million. One more, and Missy would have confessed everything. She was worked up to it. She was in continual terror of an immediate exposure. Her better nature was touched and cauterised with shame for the sweet affection of which she had cheated this simple old man. She would tell him everything now and here, and the mercy that filled his heart would be extended to her because she had not waited to be unmasked by another. But she paused to measure him with her eye, or, perhaps, to take a last look at him looking kindly upon her. And in that pause the door opened, making Missy jump with fright; and when it was only Arabella who entered with the lighted kerosene lamp, Missy's eyes sped back to the old man's face in time to catch a sorrowful mute reproach that went straight to her palpitating heart. She stooped without a word to help him gather up the fragments of the torn letter.

She had no further opportunity of speaking that night; and supper would have been a silent meal but for what happened as they all sat at table. All, that night, did not include John William, who was evidently spending Christmas Eve in Melbourne. There was some little talk about him. David remarked that a mail would be in with the Christmas letters, and Missy was asked whether she had not told John William to call at the post office. She had not. During her sojourn at the farm she had only once been to the post office herself; had never sent; and had been told repeatedly she was not half anxious enough about her Home letters. They told her so now. Missy generally said it was because she was so happy and at-home with them; but tonight she made no reply; and this was where they were when there came that knock at the window which made Missy spill her cocoa and otherwise display a strange state of mind.

"Who is it?" she cried. "Who do you think it is?"

"Maybe some neighbour," said Mrs. T., "to wish us the compliments o' t' season."

"If not old Father Christmas himself!" laughed David to Missy, in the wish that she should forgive herself, as he had forgiven her, for tearing up his letter. But Missy could only stare at the window-blind, behind which the knock had been repeated, and she was trembling very visibly indeed. Then the front-door opened, and it was Missy, not one of the family, that rushed out into the passage to see who it was. The family heard her shouting for joy:

"It's John William. It's only John William after all. Oh, you dear, dear old Jack!"

Very quickly she was back in the room, and down on the horsehair sofa, breathing heavily. John William followed in his town clothes.

"Yes, of course it's me. Good evening, all. Who did you think it was, Missy?"

"I thought it was visitors. What if it had been? Oh, I hate visitors, that's all."

"Then I'm sorry to hear it," remarked Mrs. Teesdale sourly, "for we have visitors coming to-morrow."

"I hate 'em, too," said John William wilfully.

"Then I'll thank you to keep your hates to yourselves," cried Mrs. T. "It's very rude of you both. Your mother wouldn't have spoke so, Missy!"

"Wouldn't she!" laughed the girl. "I wonder if you know much about my mother? But after that I think I'll be off to bed. I am rude, I know I am, but I never pretended to be anything else."

This was fired back at them from the door, and then Missy was gone without saying good-night.

"She's not like her mother," said Mrs. T. angrily; "no, that she isn't!"

"But why in the name of fortune go and tell her so?" John William blurted out. "I never knew anything like you, mother; on Christmas Eve, too!"

"I think," said David gently, "that Missy is not quite herself. She has been very excitable all day, and I think it would have been better to have taken no notice of what she said. You should remember, my dear, that she is utterly unused to our climate, and that even to us these last few days have been very trying."

Arabella was the only one who had nothing at all to say, either for Missy or against her. But she went to Missy's room a little later, and there she spoke out:

"You thought it was—Stanborough! I saw you did."

"Then I did—for the moment. But it was very silly of me—I don't know what could have put him into my head, when I've settled him so finely for good and all!"

"God bless you, Missy! But—but do you think there is any fear of him coming back and walking right in like that?"

"Not the least. Still, if he did—if he did, mark you—I'd tackle him again as soon as look at him. So never you fear, my girl, you leave him to me."

CHAPTER XI

A CHRISTMAS OFFERING

In the Melbourne shops that Christmas Eve the younger Teesdale had been perpetrating untold acts of extravagance, for two of which a certain very bad character was entirely and solely responsible. Thus with next day's Christmas dinner there was a bottle of champagne, and the healths of Mr. and Mrs. Oliver, and of Miriam their daughter, were drunk successively, and with separate honours. Missy thereat seemed to suffer somewhat from her private feelings, as indeed she did suffer, but those feelings were not exactly what they were suspected to be at the time. She was wondering how much longer she could keep up this criminal pretence and act this infamous part. And as she wondered, a delirious recklessness overcame her, and emptying her glass she jumped to her feet to confess to them all then and there; but the astonished eye of Mrs. Teesdale went like cold steel to her heart, and she wished them long life and prosperity instead. She found herself seated once more with a hammering heart and sensations that drove her to stare hard at the old woman's unsympathetic face, as her own one chance of remaining cool till the end of the meal. And yet a worse moment was to follow hard upon the last.

Missy had made straight for the nearest and the thickest shelter, which happened to underlie that dark jagged rim of river-timber at which old Teesdale was so fond of gazing. She had thrown herself face downward on a bank beside the sluggish brown stream; her fingers were interwoven under her face, her thumbs stuck deep into her ears. So she did not hear the footsteps until they were close beside her, when she sat up suddenly with a face of blank terror.

It was only John William. "Who did you think it was?" said he, smiling as he sat down beside her.

Missy was trembling dreadfully. "How was I to know?" she answered nervously. "It might have been a bushranger, mightn't it?"

"Well, hardly," replied John William, as seriously as though the question had been put in the best of good faith. And it now became obvious that he also had something on his mind and nerves, for he shifted a little further away from Missy, and sat frowning at the dry brown grass, and picking at it with his fingers.

"Anyhow, you startled me," said Missy, as she arranged the carroty fringe that had been shamefully dishevelled a moment before. "I am very easily startled, you see."

"I am very sorry. I do apologise, I'm sure! And I'll go away again this minute, Missy, if you like." He got to his knees with the words, which were spoken in a more serious tone than ever.

"Oh, no, don't go away. I was only moping. I am glad you've come."

"Thank you, Missy."

"But now you have come, you've got to talk and cheer me up. See? There's too many things to think about on a Christmas Day—when—when you're so far away from everybody."

John William agreed and sympathised. "The fact is I had something to show you," he added; "that's why I came."

"Then show away," said Missy, forcing a smile. "Something in a cardboard box, eh?"

"Yes. Will you open it and tell me how you like it?" He handed her the box that he had taken out of his breast-pocket. Missy opened it and produced a very yellow bauble of sufficiently ornate design.

"Well, I'm sure! A bangle!"

"Yes; but what do you think of it?" asked John William anxiously. He had also blushed very brown.

"Oh, of course I think it's beautiful—beautiful!" exclaimed Missy, with unmistakable sincerity. "But who's it for? That's what I want to know," she added, as she scanned him narrowly.

"Can't you guess?"

"Well, let's see. Yes—you're blushing! It's for your young woman, that's evident."

John William edged nearer.

"It's for the young lady—the young lady I should like to be mine—only I'm so far below her," he began in a murmur. Then he looked at her hard. "Missy, for God's sake forgive me," he cried out, "but it's for you!"

"Nonsense!"

"But I mean it. I got it last night. Do, please, have it."

"No," said Missy firmly. "Thank you ever so very awfully much; but you must take it back." And she held it out to him with a still hand.

"I can't take it back—I won't!" cried young Teesdale excitedly. "Consider it only as a Christmas box—surely your father's godson may give you a little bit of a Christmas box? That's me, Missy, and anything else I've gone and said you must forgive and forget too, for it was all a slip. I didn't mean to say it, Missy, I didn't indeed. I hope I know my position better than that. But this here little trumpery what-you-call-it, you must accept it as a Christmas present from us all. Yes, that's what you must do; for I'm bothered if I take it back."

"You must," repeated Missy very calmly. "I think you mean to break my heart between you with your kindness. Here's the box and here's the bangle."

John William looked once and for all into the resolute light eyes. Then first he took the box and put the lid on it, and stowed it away in his breastpocket; and after that he took that gold bangle, very gingerly, between finger and thumb, and spun it out into the centre of the brown river, where it made bigger, widening bangles, that took the best part of a minute to fail and die away. Then everything was stiller than before; and stillest of all were the man and the woman who stood facing each other on the bank, speckled with the steep sunlight that came down on them like rain through the leaves of the river-timber overhead.

"That was bad," said Missy at last. "Something else was worse. It's not much good your trying to hedge matters with me; and for my part I'm going to speak straight and plain for once. If I thought that you'd gone and fallen in love with me—as sure as we're standing here, Jack, I'd put myself where you've put that bangle."

Her hand pointed to the place. There was neither tremor in the one nor ripple upon the other.

"But why?" Teesdale could only gasp.

"Because I'm so far below you."

"Missy! Missy!" he was beginning passionately, but she checked him at once.

"Let well alone, Jack. I've spoken God's truth. I'm not going to say any more; only when you know all about me—as you may any day now—perhaps even to-day—don't say that I told nothing but lies. That's all. Now must I go back to the house, or will you?"

He glanced towards the river with unconscious significance. She shook her head and smiled. He hung his, and went away.

Once more Missy was alone among the river-timber; once more she flung herself down upon the short, dry grass, but this time upon her back, while her eyes and her ears were wide open.

A cherry-picker was frivolling in the branches immediately above her. From the moment it caught her eye, Missy seemed to take great interest in that cherry-picker's proceedings. She had wasted innumerable cartridges on these small birds, but that was in her blood-thirsty days, now of ancient history, and there had never been any ill-feeling between Missy and the cherry-pickers even then. One solitary native cat was all the fair game that she had slaughtered in her time. She now took to wondering why it was that these animals were never to be seen upon a tree in day-time; and as she wondered, her eyes hunted all visible forks and boughs; and as she hunted, a flock of small parrots came whirring like a flight of arrows, and called upon Missy's cherry-picker, and drove him from the branches overhead. But the parrots were a new interest, and well worth watching. They had red beaks and redder heads and tartan wings and emerald breasts. Missy had had shots at these also formerly; even now she shut her left eye and pretended that her right fore-finger was a gun, and felt certain of three fine fellows with one barrel had it really been a gun. Then at last she turned on her elbow towards the river, and opened her mouth to talk to herself. And after a long half-hour with nature this was all she had to say:

"If I did put myself in there, what use would it be? That beast would get a hold of Arabella then. But it'd be nice never to know what they said when they found out everything. What's more, I'd rather be in there, after this, than in any town. After this!"

She gave that mob of chattering parrots a very affectionate glance; also the dark green leaves with the dark blue sky behind them; also the brown, still river, hidden away from the sun. She had come to love them all, and the river would be a very good place for her indeed.

She muttered on: "Then to think of John William! Well, I never! It would be best for him too if I snuffed out, one way or another; and as for 'Bella, if that brute doesn't turn up soon, he may not turn up at all. But he said he'd keep me waiting. He's low enough down to do it, too."

She looked behind her shuddering, as she had looked behind her many and many a time during the last few days. Instantly her eyes fell upon that at which one has a right to shudder. Within six feet of Missy a brown snake had stiffened itself from the ground with darting tongue and eyes like holes in a head full of fire. And Missy began to smile and hold out her hands to it.

"Come on," she said. "Come on and do your worst! I wish you would. That'd be a way out without no blame to anybody—and just now they might be sorry. Come on, or I'll come to you. Ah, you wretch, you blooming coward, you!"

She had got to her knees, and was actually making for the snake on all fours; but it darted back into its hole like a streak of live seaweed; and Missy then rose wearily to her feet, and stood looking around her once more, as though for the last time.

"What am I to do?" she asked of river, trees, and sky. "What am I to do? I haven't the pluck to finish myself, nor yet to make a clean breast. I haven't any pluck at all. I might go back and do something that'd make the whole kit of 'em glad to get rid o' me. That's what I call a gaudy idea, but it would mean clearing out in a hurry. And I don't want to clear out—not yet. Not just yet! So I'll slope back and see what's happening and how things are panning out; and I'll go on sitting tight as long as I'm let."

CHAPTER XII

"THE SONG OF MIRIAM"

Accordingly Missy reappeared in the verandah about tea-time, and in the verandah she was once more paralysed with the special terror that was hanging over her from hour to hour in these days. An unfamiliar black coat had its back to the parlour window; it was only when Missy discerned an equally unfamiliar red face at the other side of the table that she remembered that Christmas visitors had been expected in the afternoon, and reflected that these must be they. The invited guests were a brace of ministers connected with the chapel attended by the Teesdales, and the red face, which was also very fat, and roofed over with a thatch of very white hair, rose out of as black a coat as that other of which Missy had seen the back. So these were clearly the ministers. And they were already at tea.

As soon as Missy entered the parlour she recognised the person sitting with his back to the window. He had lantern jaws hung with black whiskers, and a very long but not so very cleanshaven upper lip. His name was Appleton, he was the local minister, and Missy had not only been taken to hear him preach, but she had met him personally, and made an impression, judging by the length of time the ministers hand had rested upon her shoulder on that occasion. He greeted her now in a very complimentary manner, and with many seasonable wishes, which received the echo of an echo from the elder reverend visitor, whom Mrs. Teesdale made known to Missy as their old friend Mr. Crowdy.

"Mr. Crowdy," added Mrs. T., reproachfully, "came all the way from Williamtown to preach our Christmas morning sermon. It was a beautiful sermon, if ever I heard one."

"It was that," put in David, wagging his kind old head. "But you should have told Mr. Crowdy, my dear, how Miriam feels our heat. I wouldn't let her go this morning, Mr. Crowdy, on that account. So you see it's me that's to blame."

Mr. Crowdy looked very sorry for Miriam, but very well pleased with himself and the world. Missy was shooting glances of gratitude at her indefatigable old champion. Mr. Crowdy began to eye her kindly out of his fat red face.

"So your name's Miriam? A good old-fashioned Biblical name, is Miriam," he said, in a wheezy, plethoric voice. "Singular thing, too, my name's Aaron; but I'd make an oldish brother for you, young lady, hey?"

Miriam laughed without understanding, and showed this. So Mr. Teesdale explained.

"Miriam, my dear, was the sister of Moses and Aaron, you remember."

Missy did remember.

"Moses and Aaron? Why, of course!" cried she. "'Says Moses to Aaron! '"

The quotation was not meant to go any further; but the white-haired minister asked blandly, "Well, what did he say?" So bland, indeed, was the question that Missy hummed forth after a very trifling hesitation—

"Says Moses to Aaron,

While talking of these times'—

Says Aaron to Moses,

'I vote we make some rhymes!

The ways of this wicked world,

'Tis not a bed of roses—

No better than it ought to be—'

'Right you are!' says Moses."

There was a short but perfect silence, during which Mrs. Teesdale glared at Missy and her husband looked pained. Then the old minister simply remarked that he saw no fun in profanity, and John William (who was visibly out of his element) felt frightfully inclined to punch Mr. Crowdy's white head for him. But the Reverend Mr. Appleton took a lighter view of the matter.

"With all due deference to our dear old friend," said this gentleman, with characteristic unction, "I must say that I am of opinion 'e is labouring under a slight misconception. Miss Miriam, I feel sure, was not alluding to any Biblical characters at all, but to two typical types of the latter-day Levite. Miss Miriam nods! I knew that I was right!"

"Then I was wrong," said Mr. Crowdy, cheerfully, as he nodded to Missy, who had not seriously aggrieved him; "and all's well that ends well."

"Hear, hear!" chimed in David, thankfully. "Mrs. T., Mr. Appleton's cup's off. And Mr. Crowdy hasn't got any jam. Or will you try our Christmas cake now, Mr. Crowdy? My dears, my dears, you're treating our guests very shabbily!"

"Some of them puts people about so—some that ought to know better," muttered Mrs. Tees-dale under her breath; but after that the tea closed over Missy's latest misdemeanour—if indeed it was one for Missy—and a slightly sticky meal went as smoothly as could be expected to its end.

Then Mr. Appleton said grace, and Mr. Crowdy, pushing back his plate and his chair, exclaimed in an oracular wheeze, "The Hundred!"

"The Old 'Undredth," explained the other, getting on his feet and producing a tuning-fork. He was the musical minister, Mr. Appleton. Nevertheless, he led them off too high or too low, and started them afresh three times, before they were all standing round that tea-table and singing in unison at the rate of about two lines per minute—

"All—peo—ple—that—on—earth—do—dwell—
Sing—to—the—Lord—with—cheer-fill-voice-
Him—serve—with—fear—His—praise-forth-tell-
Come—ye—be—fore—Him—and—re-joice."

And so through the five verses, which between them occupied the better part of ten minutes; whereafter Mr. Crowdy knelt them all down with their elbows among the tea-things, and offered up a prayer.

Now it is noteworthy that the black sheep of this mob, that had no business to be in this mob at all, displayed no sort of inclination to smile at these grave proceedings. They took Missy completely by surprise; but they failed to tickle her sense of humour, because there was too much upon the conscience which had recently been born again to Missy's soul. On the contrary, the hymn touched her heart and the prayer made it bleed; for that heart was become like a foul thing cleaned in the pure atmosphere of this peaceful homestead. The prayer was very long and did not justify its length. It comprised no point, no sentence, which in itself could have stung a sinner to the quick. But through her fingers Missy could see the bald pate, the drooping eyelids, and the reverent, submissive expression of old Mr. Teesdale. And they drew the blood. The girl rose from her knees with one thing tight in her mind. This was the fixed determination to undeceive that trustful nature without further delay than was necessary, and in the first fashion which offered.

A sort of chance came almost immediately; it was not the best sort, but Missy had grown so desperate that now she was all for running up her true piratical colours and then sheering off before a gun could be brought to bear upon her. So she seized the opportunity which occurred in the best parlour, to which the party adjourned after tea. The best parlour was very seldom used. It had the fusty smell of all best parlours, which never are for common use, and was otherwise too much of a museum of albums, antimacassars, ornaments and footstools, to be a very human habitation at its best. Though all that met the eye looked clean, there was a strong pervading sense of the dust of decades; but some of this was about to be raised.

In the passage Mr. Appleton had taken Missy most affectionately by the arm, and had whispered of Mr. Crowdy, who was ahead, "A grand old man, and ripe for 'eaven!" But as they entered the best parlour he was complimenting Missy upon her voice, which had quite altered the sound of the late hymn from the moment when John William fetched and handed to her an open hymn-book. And here Mr. Crowdy, seating himself in the least uncomfortable of the antimacassared chairs, had his say also.

"I like your voice too," the florid old minister observed, cocking a fat eye at Miriam. "But it is only natural that any young lady of your name should be musical. Surely you remember? 'And Miriam the prophetess, the sister of Aaron, took a timbrel in her hand; and all the women went out after her with timbrels and with dances—' and so forth. Exodus fifteen. I suppose you can't play upon the timbrel, hey, Miss Miriam?"

"No," said Missy; "but I can dance."

"Hum! And sing? What I mean is, young lady, do you only sing hymns?"

Missy kept her countenance.

"I have sung songs as well," she ventured to assert.

"Then give us one now, Missy," cried old Tees-dale. "That's what Mr. Crowdy wants, and so do we all."

"Something lively?" suggested Missy, looking doubtfully at the red-faced minister.

"Lively? To be sure," replied Mr. Crowdy. "Christmas Day, young lady, is not like a Sunday unless it happens to fall on one, which I'm glad it hasn't this year. Make it as lively as convenient. I like to be livened up!" And the old man rubbed his podgy hands and leant forward in the least uncomfortable chair.

"And shall I give you a dance too?"

"A dance, by all means, if you dance alone. I understand that such dancing has become quite the rage in the drawing-rooms at home. And a very good thing too, if it puts a stop to that dancing two together, which is an abomination in the sight of the Lord. But a dance by yourself—by all manner of means!" cried Mr. Crowdy, snatching off his spectacles and breathing upon the lenses.

"But I should require an accompaniment."

"Nothing easier. My friend Appleton can accompany anything that is hummed over to him twice. Can't you, Appleton?"

"Mr. Crowdy," replied the younger man, in an injured voice, as he looked askance at a little old piano with its back to the wall, and still more hopelessly at a music-stool from which it would be perfectly impossible to see the performance; "Mr. Crowdy, I do call this unfair! I—I—"

"You—you—I know you, sir!" cried the aged divine, with unmerciful good-humour. "Haven't I heard you do as much at your own teas? Get up at once, sir, and don't shame our cloth by disobliging a young lady who is offering to sing to us in the latest style from England!"

"I'm not offering, mind!" said Missy a little sharply. "Still, I'm on to do my best. Come over here, Mr. Appleton, and I'll hum it quite quietly in your ear. It goes something like this."

That conquered Appleton; but the Teesdales, while leaving the whole matter in the hands of Missy and of the venerable Mr. Crowdy, who wanted to hear her sing, had thrown in words here and there in favour of the performance and of Mr. Appleton's part in it; all except Mrs. T., who was determined to have no voice in a matter of which she hoped to disapprove, and who showed her determination by an even more unsympathetic cast of countenance than was usual with her wherever Missy was concerned. Mrs. T. was seated upon a hard sofa by her husband's side, Arabella on a low footstool, John William by the window, and the two ministers we know where. The one at the piano seemed to have got his teeth into a banjo accompaniment which would have sounded very wonderfully like a banjo on that little old tin-pot piano if he had thumped not quite so hard; but now Missy was posing in front of the mantelpiece, and all eyes but the unlucky accompanist's were covering her eagerly.

"Now you're all right, Mr. Appleton. You keep on like that, and I'll nip in when I'm ready. If I stop and do a spout between the verses you can stop too, only don't forget to weigh in with the chorus. But when I dance, you keep on. See? That'll be all right, then. Ahem!"

Missy had spoken behind her hand in a stage whisper; now she turned to her audience and struck an attitude that made them stare. The smile upon her face opened their eyes still wider—it was so brazen, so insinuating, and yet so terribly artificial. And with that smile she began to dance, very slowly and rhythmically, plucking at her dress and showing her ankles, while Appleton thumped carefully on, little knowing what he was missing. And when it seemed as though no song was coming the song began.

But the dance went on through all, being highly appropriate, at all events to verse one, which ran:—

"Yuss! A fling and a slide with a pal, inside,
It isn't 'alf bad—but mind you!
The spot for a 'op is in front o' the shop
With a fried-fish-breeze be'ind you...
Well! Every lass was bold as brass,
But divvle a one a Venus;
An' Rorty 'Arry as I'm to marry
The only man between us!"

Here Missy and the music stopped together, Mr. Appleton holding his fingers in readiness over the next notes, while Missy interrupted her dance, too, to step forward and open fire upon her audience in the following prose:—

"Now that's just 'ow the 'ole thing 'appened. They wouldn't give my pore 'Arry no peace—catch them! Well, 'Arry 'e done 's level—I will say that for 'im. 'E took on three at once; but 'is legs wouldn't go round fast enough, an' 'is arms wouldn't go round at all—catch them! Now would you believe it? When 'e's 'ad enough o' the others—a nasty common low lot they was, too—'e 'as the cheek to come to yours truly. But—catch me! 'No, 'Arry,' I sez, 'ere's 2d. to go and 'ave a pint o' four-'.If,' I sez, 'w'ich you must need it,' I sez—just like that. So 'e goes an' 'as 'alf a dozen. That's my 'Arry all over, that is! An' w'en 'e come back 'e 'as the impidence to ax me again. But I give 'im a look like this," cried Missy, leering horribly at the venerable Crowdy. "Such a look! Just like that"—with a repetition of the leer for Mrs. Teesdale's special benefit—"'.ause I seen what was wrong with 'im in the twinkling of a dress-improver. An' after that—chorus-up, Mr. Appleton!—why, after that—

"'Arry 'e 'ad the 'ump,
An' I lets 'im know it—plump
'E swore 'e'd not,

So 'e got it 'ot,
I caught 'im a good ole crump.
You should 'a' seen 'im jump!
I didn't give a dump!
For I yells to 'is pals
'Now look at 'im, gals—
Arry, 'e 'as the 'ump!'rdquo;

The dancing had been taken up again with the chorus. There was some dancing plain at the end of it.
Then came verse two:—

"'E swore and cussed till you thought 'e'd bust,
W'ich' is 'abit is when drinky;
'E cussed and swore till 'is mouth was sore
An' the street was painted pinky.
So I sez, sez I, to a stander-by
As was standin' by to listen,
'We've 'ad quite enough o' the reg'lar rough,
An' a bit too much o' this 'un!'rdquo;

"'Yuss,'rdquo; continued Missy without a break, "'an' if you're a man,' I sez, 'come an' 'elp shift this 'ere
bloomin' imitition,' I sez. 'Right you are,' 'e sez, 'since you put it so flatterin' like. An' wot do they call
you, my dear,' sez 'e. 'That's my bloomin' business,' sez I, 'wot's yours on the charge-sheet?' 'Ted,' sez 'e.
'Right,' sez I. 'You git a holt of 'is 'eels, Ted, an' I'll 'ang on to 'is 'air!'rdquo;

Up to this point matters had proceeded without audible let or hindrance. But it appeared that at the
psychological moment now reached by the narrator the prostrate hero had regained the command of
his tongue, and the use he made of it was represented by Missy in so voluble and violent a harangue,
couched in such exceedingly strong language, and all hurled so pointedly at the heads of Mr. and Mrs.
Teesdale on the sofa opposite the fire-place, that an inevitable interruption now occurred.

"It's quite disgusting! I won't allow such language in my house. Stop at once!" cried Mrs. T. half rising;
but Missy's voice was louder; while old David stretched an arm in front of his wife and fenced her to the
sofa.

"Sit still, my dear, and don't be foolish," said he, quite firmly. "Can't you see that it's part of the song,
and only in fun?"

"Only in fun!" echoed Missy, whose speaking voice had risen to a hoarse scream. "Ho, yuss, an' I s'pose
it was fun between 'Arry an' me an' Ted? You bet your bags it wasn't! Why, time we'd done with 'im,
Ted's rigging was gone to glory—all but 'is chest-protector. And as for me, you couldn't ha' made a
decent pen-wiper out o' my 'ole attire. An' why? Why 'cause—now then, you at the pianner!—'cause—

"'Arry' e' ad the 'ump—
The liquorin' lushin' lump—
So I sez to Ted,
"Ere, sit on 'is 'ead,
Or shove 'im under the pump!'

Ted 'e turns out a trump.
We done it with bump an' thump.
For that 'orrible 'Arry
Was 'eavy to carry—
An' 'Arry 'e 'ad 'ump!"

Now not one of them guessed that this was the end of the song. They had made up their minds to more and worse, and they got it in Missy's final dance. She was wearing a dark blue skirt of some thin material. Already there had been glimpses of a white underskirt and a pair of crimson ankles, but now there were further and fuller views. John William and Arabella had been curiously and painfully fascinated from the beginning. Their father was still barring their mother to the sofa with an outstretched arm. The poor old minister sat forward in his chair with his eyes protruding from his head. His junior, who was still thumping the old piano as though his life depended upon it, was the one person present who saw nothing of what was going on; and he suspected nothing amiss; he had been too busy with his notes to attend even to the words. Every other eye was fixed upon the dancing girl; every other forehead was wet with a cold perspiration. But Mr. Appleton was so far unconsciously infected with the spirit of the proceedings that he was now playing that banjo accompaniment at about double his rate of starting. And the ornaments were rattling on mantelpiece and table and bracket, and a small vase fell with a crash into the fender—Missy had brought it down with the toe of one high-heeled shoe. Then with a whoop she was at the door. The door was flung open. There was a flutter of white and a flare of crimson, neither quite in the room nor precisely in the passage. The door was slammed, and the girl gone.

Mr. Teesdale was the first to rise. His face was very pale and agitated. He crossed the room and laid a hand upon the shoulder of Mr. Appleton, who was still pounding with all his heart at the old piano. Appleton stopped and revolved on the music-stool with a face of very comical ignorance and amazement. Mr. Teesdale went on to the door and turned the handle. It did not open. The key had been turned upon the outer side.

CHAPTER XIII

ON THE VERANDAH

Night had fallen, and Mr. Teesdale had the homestead all to himself. Arabella and her mother had accompanied the ministers to evening worship in the township chapel. John William was busy with the milking. As for Missy, she had disappeared, as well she might, after her outrageous performance in the best parlour. And Mr. Teesdale was beginning to wonder whether they were ever to see her again; and if never, then what sort of report could he send his old friend now?

He did not know. Her last prank was also incomparably her worst, it had stunned poor David, and it left him unable to think coherently of Missy any longer. Yet her own father had warned him that Miriam was a very modern type of young woman; had hinted at the possibility of her startling simple folks. Then again, David, who took his newspaper very seriously indeed, had his own opinion of modern society in England and elsewhere. And if, as he believed, Missy was a specimen of that society, then it was not right to be hard upon the specimen. Had not he gathered long ago from the newspapers that the music-hall song and dance had found their way into smart London drawing-rooms? Now that he had heard that song, and seen that dance, were they much worse than he had been led to suppose? If so, then society was even blacker than it was painted, that was all. The individual in any case was not to blame, but least of all in this case, where the individual had shown nothing but kindness to an uninteresting old man, quite aside and apart from her position in the old man's house as the child of his earliest friend.

And yet—and yet—he would do something to blot this last lurid scene out of his mind. There was nothing he would not do, if only he could do that. Yet this only showed him the narrowness of his own mind. That, after all, was half the trouble. Here at the antipodes, in an overlooked corner that had missed development with the colony, just as Mr. Teesdale himself had missed it: here all minds must be narrow. But theirs at the farm were perhaps narrower than most; otherwise they would never have been so shocked at Missy; at all events they would not have shown their feelings, as they evidently must have shown them, to have driven poor Missy off the premises, as they had apparently done.

Mr. Teesdale became greatly depressed as he made these reflections, and gradually got as much of the blame on to his own shoulders as one man could carry. It was very dark. He was sitting out on the verandah and smoking; but it was too dark to enjoy a pipe properly, even if David could have enjoyed anything just then. He was sitting in one of those wooden chairs in which he had so often sat of late while Missy read to him, and one hand rested mournfully upon the seat of the empty chair at his side. Not that he as yet really dreaded never seeing Missy again. He was keeping a look-out for her all the time. Sooner or later she was bound to come back.

She had come back already, but it was so dark that David never saw her until he was putting a light to his second pipe. Then the face of Missy, with her red hair tousled, came out of the night beyond the verandah with startling vividness, and it was the most defiant face that ever David Tees-dale had beheld.

"Missy," cried he, "is that you?"

He dropped the match and Missy's face was gone.

"Yes, it's me," said her voice, in such a tone as might have been expected from her face.

"Then come in, child, come in," said David joyfully, pushing back his chair as he rose. "I'm that glad you've come back, you can't think!"

"But I haven't come back—that's just it," answered the defiant voice out of the night.

"Then I'm going to fetch you back, Missy. I'm going—"

"You stop in that verandah. If you come out I'll take to my heels and you'll never see me again—never! Now look here, Mr. Teesdale, haven't I sickened you this time?"

"Done what, Missy?" asked David, uneasily, from the verandah. He could see her outline now.

"Sickened you. I should have thought I'd sickened you just about enough this trip, if you'd asked me. I should have said I'd choked you off for good and all."

"You know you've done no such thing, Missy. What nonsense the child will talk!"

"What! I didn't sicken you this afternoon?"

"No."

"Didn't disgust you, if you like that better?"

"No."

"Didn't make you perspire, the whole lot of you?"

"Of course you didn't, Missy. How you talk! You amused us a good deal, and you surprised us, too, a bit; but that was all."

"Oh! So that was all, was it? So I only surprised you a bit? I suppose you don't happen to know whether it was a big bit, eh?"

But David now decided that the time was come for firmness.

"Listen to me, Missy; I'm not going to have any more to say to you unless you come inside at once!"

"But what if I'm not never coming inside—never no more?"

There was that within the words which made David pause to consider. At length he said: "Very well, then, come into the verandah and we'll have a sensible talk here, and I won't force you into the house; though where else you're to go I don't quite see. However, come here, and I won't insist on your coming a step further."

"Honour bright?"

"Of course."

"Hope to die?"

"I don't understand you, Missy; but I meant what I said."

"Then I'm coming. One moment, though! Is anybody about? Is Mrs. Teesdale in the house?"

"No, she's gone to chapel. So has Arabella, and John William's milking. They'll none of 'em be back just yet. Ah, that's better, my dear girl, that's better!"

Missy was back in her old wooden chair. Mr. Teesdale sat down again in its fellow and put his hand affectionately upon the girl's shoulder.

"So you mean to tell me your hairs didn't stand on end!" said Missy, in a little whisper that was as unnecessary as it was fascinating just then.

"I haven't got much to boast of," answered the old man cheerily; "but what hair I have didn't do any such thing, Missy."

"Now just you think what you're saying," pursued the girl, with an air as of counsel cautioning a witness. "You tell me I neither sickened you, nor disgusted you, nor choked you off for good and all with that song and dance I gave you this afternoon. Your hairs didn't stand on end, and I didn't even make you perspire—so you say! But do you really mean me to believe you?"

"Why, bless the child! To be sure—to be sure!"

"Then, Mr. Teesdale, I must ask you whether you're in the habit of telling lies."

David opened his mouth to answer very promptly indeed, but kept it open without answering at all at the moment. He had remembered something that sent his left thumb and forefinger of their own accord into an empty waistcoat pocket. "No," said he presently with a sigh, "I'm not exactly in the habit of saying what isn't true."

"But you do it sometimes?"

"I have done it, God forgive me! But who has not?"

"Not me," cried Missy candidly. "There's not a bigger liar in this world than me! I'm going to tell you about that directly. I'm so glad you've told a lie or two yourself—it gives me such a leg-up—though I never should have thought it of you, Mr. Teesdale. I've told hundreds since I've known you. Have you told any since you've known me?"

The question was asked with all the inquisitive sympathy of one discovering a comrade in sin. "I mean not counting the ones you've just been telling me," added Missy when she got no answer, "about your not being shocked, and all the rest of it."

"That was no falsehood, Missy; that was the truth."

"All right, then, we'll pass that. Have you told any other lies since I've been here? Just whisper, and I promise I won't let on. I do so want to know."

"But why, my dear—but why?"

"Because it'll be ever so much easier for me to make my confession when you've made yours."

"Your confession! What can you have to confess, Missy?" The old man chuckled as he patted her hand.

"More than you're prepared for. But you must fire first. Have you or have you not told a wicked story since I've been staying here?"

Mr. Teesdale cleared his throat and sat upright in his chair.

"Missy," said he solemnly, "the only untruth I can remember telling in all my life, I have told since you have been with us; and I've told it over and over again. Heaven knows why I admit this much to you! I suppose there's something in you, my dear, that makes me say' more than ever I mean to say. But I'm not going to say another word about this—that's flat."

"Good Lord!" murmured Missy. "And you've told it over and over and over again! Oh, do tell me," she whispered coaxingly; "you might."

"My dear, I've told you too much already." And old Teesdale would have risen and paced the verandah, but a pair of strong arms restrained him. They were Missy's arms thrown round his neck, and the old man was content to sit still.

"Tell me one thing," she wheedled softly: "had it anything to do with me—that wicked story you've told so often?"

Mr. Teesdale was silent.

"Then it had something to do with me. Let me think. Had it anything—to do with—your watch?... Then it had! And anything to do with that twenty pounds you sent me to the post office?... Yes, it had! You pawned that watch to get me that money. You said you had left it mending. I've heard you say so a dozen times. So this is the lie you meant you'd told over and over again. And all for me! O Mr. Teesdale, I am so sorry—I am—so—sorry."

She had broken down and was sobbing bitterly on his shoulder. The old man stroked her head.

"You needn't take it so to heart, Missy dear. Nay, come! Shall I tell you why? Because it wasn't all for you, Missy. I hardly knew you then. Nay, honey, it was all for your dear father—no one else."

The effect of this distinction, made with a very touching sort of pride, was to withdraw Missy's arms very suddenly from the old man's neck, and to leave her sitting and trembling as far away from him as possible, though still in her chair. Her moment was come; but her nerve and her courage, her coolness and steadiness of purpose, where were they now?

She braced herself together with a powerful effort. Hours ago she had resolved, under influences that may be remembered, to undeceive the too trustful old man now at her side. To that resolve she still adhered; but as it had since become evident that nothing she could possibly do would lead him to suspect the truth, there was now no way for her but the hardest way of all—that of a full and clean confession. Her teeth were chattering when she began, but Mr. Teesdale understood her to say:

"Before you told your lie I had told you a dozen—I spoke hardly a word of truth all the way into Melbourne that day. But there was one great, big, tremendous lie at the bottom of all the rest. And can't you guess what that was? You must guess—I can never tell you—I couldn't get it out."

Mr. Teesdale was very silent. "Yes, I think I can guess," he said at last, and sadly enough.

"Then what was it?" exclaimed Missy in an eager whisper. She was shivering with excitement.

"Well, my dear, I suppose it was to do with them friends you had to meet at the theatre. You might have trusted me a bit more, Missy! I shouldn't have thought so much of it, after all."

"Of what?"

"Why, of your going to the theatre alone. Wasn't that it, Missy?"

The girl moaned. "Oh, no—no! It was something ever so much worse than that."

"Then you weren't stopping with friends at all. Was that it? Yes, you were staying all by yourself at one of the hotels."

"No—no—no. It was ever so much worse than that too. That was one of the lies I told you, but it was nothing like the one I mean."

"Missy," old David said gravely, "I don't want to know what you mean. I don't indeed! I'd far rather know nothing at all about it."

"But you must know!" cried Missy in desperation.

"Why must I?"

"Because this has gone on far too long. And I never meant it to go on at all. No, I give you my oath I only meant to have a lark in the beginning—to have a lark and be done with it! Anyhow I can't keep it up any longer; that's all about it, and—but surely you can guess now, Mr. Teesdale, can't you?"

Again the old man was long in answering. "Yes," he exclaimed at length, and with such conviction in his voice that Missy grasped her chair-arms tight and sat holding her breath. "Yes, I do see now. You borrowed that money not because you really needed it, but because—"

The girl's groans stopped him. "To think that you can't guess," she wailed, "though I've as good as told you in so many words!"

"No, I can't guess," answered David decisively. "What's more, I don't want to. So I give it up. Hush, Missy, not another word! I won't have it! I'll put my fingers in my ears if you will persist. I don't care whether it's true or whether it isn't, I'm not going to sit here and listen to you pitching into yourself when—when—"

"When what?"

"Why, when I've grown that fond of you, my dear!"

"And are you fond of me?" said Missy, in a softened voice that quivered badly. She put her arms once more round the old man's neck, and let her tousled head rest again upon his shoulder. "Are you really so fond of me as all that?"

"My dear, we all are. You know that as well as I do."

Missy made one important exception in her own mind, but not aloud. Kind, worn fingers were now busy with her hair, now patting her shoulder tenderly; and in all her poor life Missy had never known a father or a father's love. Even with the will she could not have spoken for some minutes. When she did speak next it was to echo the old man's last words; "Yes, I know that as well as you do. And I know how it hurts! But tell me, can you possibly be as fond of me after this afternoon?"

"I can," said old Teesdale. "I can only speak for myself. Maybe I think more of you than anyone else does; I've seen more of you, and had more of your kindness. Nothing could make me forget that, Missy—how you've sat with me, and walked with me, and read to me, and taken notice of the old man, no matter who else was by or who wasn't. No, I could never forget all that, my dear; nothing that you could do could make me forget one half of that!"

"And nothing that I have done?"

"Still less anything that you have done."

"But if you found out that I'd been deceiving you all along, and obtained every mortal thing on false pretences, and taken the filthiest advantage of your kindness—surely that would wipe out any little good turns which anybody would have done you? Of course it would!"

"It might. But anybody wouldn't have done 'em—anybody wouldn't," the old man said, leaving a kiss upon the hair between his fingers. "At all events, Missy, there's one thing that nothing could blot out; for whatever you did, you'd still be your dear father's daughter!"

Very slowly and deliberately, Missy unwound her arms and lifted her head, and got out of the chair, and stood to her full height in the dark verandah.

"That's just it," she said calmly, distinctly. "That's just what I was coming to."

But Mr. Teesdale had also risen, and he was not listening to Missy. For footsteps were drawing near through the grass—footsteps and the rustle of stiff Sunday gowns, and the creaking of comfortless Sunday boots—and a harsh voice was crying more harshly than was even its wont:

"Is that you, David? And is that Miriam beside you? And how dare she come back and show her face, I wonder? Ay, that's what I want to know!"

David ran to meet and expostulate with his harder half. It was seldom that he even tried to quell that outspoken tongue; but now he both tried and succeeded, though Missy in the verandah could not hear by how much artifice or in what words. In another minute, however, Mr. Teesdale was again at her side, while his wife and daughter went past them and into the house without further parley.

These few words were then exchanged in the verandah:

"Missy, she didn't mean it. You'll hear no more about it—not a word from anybody."

"I deserve to, nevertheless."

"So you'll come in, won't you, and have your supper like a dear good girl?"

"Ah, yes, I'll come in now."

"I was so afraid—Mrs. T. is that hasty and plain-spoken—that what she said might make you say you'd never come into our house any more."

"Not it," said Missy with a laugh. "That's the sort of thing to have the very opposite effect upon you. Come on in!"

CHAPTER XIV

A BOLT FROM THE BLUE

Mr. Teesdale sat at his end of the old green tablecloth, reading a singularly unseasonable communication from that middle-man who bought the milk but was never in a position to pay for it. The time was half-past eleven in the forenoon of Boxing Day, and the daily delivery of letters had just taken place. It was naturally a little later than usual, but Mr. Teesdale wished with all his heart that there had been no delivery at all. At length he raised a tired face from his bad news, and let his eyes rest for the comfort of his spirit upon the red head and fringe of his solitary companion in the parlour. Missy was seated on the sofa, and all of her but the top of her head and the bottom of her dress, with a finger or two of each hand, was hidden behind the Argus newspaper. Missy always liked to see the Argus as soon as it came, though by that time it was never less than a day old, because Mr. Teesdale had it from a friend when the friend was done with it. This morning, as usual, he had handed it to the girl before opening his letters. He now sat staring absently at the girl's hair, and was therefore somewhat slow to notice that the narrow strip of forehead under the fringe was gone so white that it was difficult to tell where paper ended and forehead began. No sooner had David seen this, however, than he saw also the paper jumping up and down in the girl's grasp; whereupon the unpleasant letter in his own hands went straightway out of his head.

"Missy," he cried, "what's the matter, my dear? What have you seen?"

Missy dashed down the paper and was on her feet in an instant. There was extraordinary spirit in the action, and her eyes were very bright.

"What have I seen?" she repeated, in a tone that suppressed excitement rather than concern. "Nothing; that is, nothing that could interest any of you; only something about a friend of mine."

Yet she bounced out of the room without another word, and forthwith went in search of Arabella.

She found her in the dairy, which was half under the ground, and wholly out of the way.

"Arabella," she cried wildly, "put down that bowl and shake hands. We're safe!"

Now Arabella was not a person of quick perceptions. She was imaginative, she was inquisitive, she had a romantic side which had very nearly been the ruin of her at the responsible age of thirty-two. Like the parent whom she so strongly resembled in her undiscerning nature and easygoing temperament, she was sufficiently credulous, weak, and unwise in her generation. On the other hand, she was by no means without her father's merits. She had the same talent for affection, the same positive genius for uncommon gratitude. She could never make light of a good turn, not even in her own mind; nor out of her own mouth could she make too much of one. In the family circle she had been very silent and subdued during these last days, but to Missy in private she had opened a contrite and a very grateful heart more times than the other had liked to listen. Vague doubts and suspicions of Missy she had entertained in the beginning; she might have them still; nay, they might well be stronger than ever, after yesterday.

But one thing was now certain concerning these shy misgivings; they might rise to the mind, but they would never again pass the lips. No matter what Missy did or said, henceforth, Arabella would shield her with all the ingenuity at her command: which was not a little: only it was sometimes hindered by a certain slowness to perceive which frequently accompanies a constitutional readiness to imagine. So when Missy wanted her to shake hands because they were safe, Arabella looked perfectly blank.

"How are we safe?" she asked. "What are we safe from?"

"Why, from your friend."

"My friend? Ah!" She understood now.

"Yes, he won't trouble us much more," pursued Missy, sidling rhythmically from one foot to the other, while her eyes lit up the dairy. "O 'Bella, 'Bella, if you knew how I feel—"

"Stop a moment," said Arabella, white as the milk that she had spilled in her agitation; "is he—is he—dead?"

"Dead? I wish he was. No, no; he's only in prison."

"In prison?"

"Yes; run in the day before Christmas Eve—the day after I swep' him out o' this—no, the very day itself. See where you'd ha' been! 'Bella, 'Bella, let's drink his health in a pint of cream! It seems too good to be true."

But Arabella was grasping with both hands the shelf which supported the bowls of milk for creaming, and her face was drawn and wretched.

"Don't, Missy!" she exclaimed with tears in her voice. "You wouldn't if you knew how sorry I am. What is he in prison for? What has he been doing?"

"Writing a cheque he had no business to write and getting the money. That's what it was this time. But it isn't the first time; no, don't you believe it."

"I am so sorry," repeated Arabella, covering her eyes.

"But why? What for?"

"For him. I—I thought I loved him."

"You thought you loved him," Missy repeated buoyantly. She was all buoyancy now. "Yes, many a girl has thought that before you, my dear. And them that thought it too long, they didn't come to think they hated him. Not they! They jolly soon knew!"

The other's wet eyes were wide open.

"How is this, Missy? You seem to know all about him. You never told me that before."

"No, I didn't. What was the use when I'd got rid of him—for the time being, anyway? I was very much afraid he'd turn up again, and I was keeping what I knew until he did. I thought it'd be time enough to tell you then; but I'll tell you now if you like. It makes no difference one way or the other, now that our friend's in quod. Very well then, as soon as ever I heard his voice that dark night I knew that I'd heard it before. Never mind where—maybe in England, maybe on the ship, maybe after I landed in Melbourne. You mustn't want to know too much. It's good enough, isn't it, that I knew what sort he was, and that when I'd known him before he was sailing under another name altogether? Yes, I thought that'd knock you! You knew Stanborough, I knew Mowbray, and the police, they've run in a man of the name of Paolo Verini, alias Thomas Stanborough, alias Paul Mowbray. 'A handsome man of foreign appearance,' the Argus says. You may look for yourself. But if that isn't good enough for you I don't know what is."

"It might be someone else for all that," murmured Arabella, shuddering at the thought of the man in prison. "Have you any other reason for making so certain that it is the same?"

"I have. I wouldn't tell you before, but now what does it matter? I've expected him turning up every hour since that night. He swore that he would; and he would have, you may depend, if he hadn't got run in."

Arabella was silent; she felt that also. She had never been able to understand how a man of so firm a purpose as her lover should have made so facile a capitulation to a mere girl like Missy. Presently she asked a question:

"Did he recognise you. Missy?"

"No," replied Missy, after a little hesitation. "No, he did not," she repeated more firmly. "And look you here,'.ella, take my advice and never give him another thought. He was a bad egg, that's what he was; you may thank your stars that he is where he is, as I thank mine."

"I can't help being sorry," sighed Arabella, wiping her eyes with her apron; "but that doesn't make me less thankful to you, Missy. You've saved me, body and soul. I was under a spell, but you broke it. I don't understand it. I can't feel it now. But God knows how I felt it then, and what would have got me but for you! So I can never be thankful enough to you, Missy, and I shall never, never be able to tell you how thankful I am."

"Then never try," said Missy lightly; "only think kindly of me when you find it a hard job. That's all you've got to try to do."

And with a light-hearted laugh and a kiss from the fingers Missy was out of the dairy and above ground in the brilliant noonday sun.

There was no one about in the yard. Missy was glad of that, because there was no living soul whom she desired to see or to speak to for hours to come. The naked sword hanging over her head had suddenly been lifted down, snapped, and thrown away; she must be alone to appreciate that. Nevertheless this should be her last day at the farm; and again, she must be alone to make the most of the last day. Alone to consider all things, especially the life lying ahead; alone to drink for the last time of the sweet sensations of this peaceful spot, and so deeply, that the taste should be with her till her dying day. Then she would depart in peace; and lastly, she must be alone to invent the why and wherefore of this departure.

So she opened the gate leading out of the yard, and going down through the gum-trees into that shallow gully, she mounted the other side, and stopped to stand in triumph under the very tree from behind which Stanborough, or Verini, had sprung and caught her in his arms. She pictured him in his cell at that moment, with only one small iron-barred square of that blue sky which was all for her; and she drew into her throat and nostrils a long draught of eucalyptus perfume. This was one of the sensations which she desired always to remember. At length, still sniffing and glancing ever at the deep blue sky above the tree-tops, yet with both eyes and ears attentive to her friends the parrots, she turned sharp to the left, crossed the road below the Cultivation, and struck into the thick of the timber on the further side.

She had shut out of her light mind every thought of penitence and remorse. There was no further occasion for her to take a serious view of the situation. The very air seemed charged with a new and most delicious sense of freedom; enough, for the present, to revel in this, without thinking of anything at all. Another comparatively new sense, that of her own iniquity, was a dead nerve for the time being. Missy was too thankful for what she had escaped to consider what she deserved; indeed, she had considered this sufficiently. On the other hand, she was enjoying a natural reaction in the most natural manner imaginable. All by herself, among the gum-trees, she burst into song, or rather the snatch of one. And on the whole one would call it unconscious song, for the snatch ran—

"You should 'a' seen 'im jump!
I didn't give a dump!
For I yells to 'is pals
'Now look at him, gals—
'Arry 'e 'as the—'"

Here it broke off. Missy halted too.

"Morning, John William," said she.

He was standing in front of her, with his gun under his arm and a dead hare in the other hand. He returned her salute gravely. Then—

"You seem very happy," he said, with a spice of bitterness.

"Oh, I haven't got it," laughed Missy, "have you?"

"Got what?"

"The 'ump."

He shook his head and grinned; as he looked at her the grin broadened.

"So I didn't shock your head off, either!" exclaimed Missy.

"Not likely. I thought it was splendid myself."

"Then why did you look so glum just now?"

"Missy, I didn't—"

"You did! I thought you'd caught the 'ump from 'Arry. I believe you have. You're looking as glum as ever again!"

It was true. But he said:

"Missy, I don't feel a bit glum."

"No?"

She was examining him coolly, critically, and he knew it.

"Not a bit!" he reiterated, hacking out a tuft of grass with his right heel. Then his miserable eyes rose fiercely upon the girl. She had been waiting for this look, however.

"You are making a great mistake," she said, "if you are imagining yourself the least little atom in love with me."

For the instant her outspokenness enraged him; then it made him meek.

"I am imagining no such thing, Missy; I know it. But I also know that it is a mistake—when you are so far above me."

"There you go! That is your mistake. It's the other way about—it's you that's so far above me. John William, if you only knew what a bad lot I am—"

"I don't care what you are."

"You don't know what I am. That's just it! I'm not what you think I am, I'm not what I make myself out to be; I'm not—I'm not!"

She was speaking passionately, being, in fact, once more on the verge of a full confession. All in a moment the impulse had come over her, and nothing could have stopped her but the thing that did. John William was not listening to a word she said; he was only gazing in her eyes.

"I don't care what you are, Missy; I shouldn't care if you were as black as sin! No, I should like it, for the blacker you were, the nearer I should be to you—the more chance I should have. If you were bad—which is all nonsense—you would still be too good for me; but I should love you, Missy, whether or no. I shall love you all my days!" He looked at her once with ravening eyes, and then spun round upon his heel. She called him back in a broken voice to tell him everything; but he shook his head without looking round, and the tree-trunks closed behind him like a door. Then Missy drew a very long breath, wiped her eyes, and sat down to think.

Her conscience was wide awake now. For an hour she let it tear and rend her. By the end of the second hour she had hardened her heart once more.

"I'm not meant to confess, that's evident," she exclaimed aloud. "I was a little fool ever to think of it."

A little fool, at that rate, she continued to be; inasmuch as for yet another hour she permitted her mind to dwell upon her attempted confessions, to old Teesdale yesterday, to John William to-day. It hurt her to think of the kindness and credulity of those two. It hurt her so much that she wept bitterly, only thinking of old David and John William his son. Yet she was thankful they had not listened, she was thankful they did not know, she was doubly thankful that she was to go away of her own accord, and without being found out after all. If she could ever make the slightest atonement! But that was for future thought.

The afternoon was well advanced when Missy once more crossed the road below the Cultivation. She was now in a perfectly philosophic frame of mind. Also she had slightly altered her plans. She would not invent an excuse for her departure; she would go without saying a word to any of them; she would run away in the night. And she would leave all her things behind her. The present value of them would not go far towards redeeming Mr. Teesdale's watch; still they must be worth something.

This she was thinking as she came to the end of the gum-trees, and opened the gate which was grown familiar to her hand and eye. Then suddenly she reflected that dinner must long be over, that she would barely be in time for tea. And the goodness of Mrs. Teesdale's tea was the next thought that filled her mind: she had the smell in her nostrils, she could almost feel the hot fluid coursing over her parched palate as she rounded the hen-yard and caught sight of the verandah. Thereat she came to a sudden standstill, and yet another new set of thoughts. The verandah was half hidden by a two-horse buggy drawn up in front of it.

"More visitors!" said Missy. "Well, I won't shock this lot. I wonder who they are? They must be swells!"

In fact, a man in livery held the reins, the afternoon sun made fireworks with the burnished harness, and the buggy was a very good one indeed.

Missy kept her eyes upon it as she approached the house. She never saw the faces that appeared for an instant at the parlour window and then disappeared. Her foot was lifted, to be set down in the verandah, when the door was flung open, and Mrs. Teesdale marched forth.

"Stand back!" she screamed. "Not another step! You would dare to set foot inside my doors again!"

Missy fell back in wonderment. As she did so a dainty-looking young lady appeared in the doorway behind Mrs. Teesdale, and screwed up her fair face at the glare of the afternoon sun. And Missy left off wondering, for in an instant she knew who that dainty-looking young lady must be.

CHAPTER XV

A DAY OF RECKONING

Missy retreated a step from the verandah, stood still, and gasped. Then she pressed both hands to her left side. She was as one walking on the down line in order to avoid the up train, only to be cut to pieces by the down express, whose very existence she had forgotten.

Her eyes fastened themselves upon one object. Presently she found that it was Mrs. Teesdale's pebble brooch. Her ears rang with a harsh, shrill voice; it took her mind some moments to capture the words and grasp their meaning.

"You wicked, wicked, ungrateful woman! To dare to come here and pass yourself off as Miriam Oliver, and live with us all these weeks—you lying hussy! If you have anything to say for yourself be sharp and say it, then out you pack!"

The convicted girl now beheld the verandah swimming with people. As her sight cleared, however, she could only count four, including Mrs. Teesdale. There was the veritable Miss Oliver, but Missy took no note of her just then. There was Arabella, white and weeping; and there was Mr. Teesdale, looking years older since the morning, with the saddest expression Missy had ever seen upon human countenance. He was gazing, not at her, but down upon the ground at her feet. John William was not there at all. Missy looked about for him very wistfully, but in vain; and her glance ended, where it had begun, upon the furious face of Mrs. Teesdale. Furious as it was, the wretched girl found it much the easiest face to meet with a firm lip and a brazen front.

"Do you know that you could be sent to prison?" Mrs. Teesdale proceeded, still at a scream. "Ay, and I'll see that you are sent, and all!"

"Nay, come!" muttered Mr. Teesdale, shaking his head at the grass, but without looking at anybody.

Then suddenly he lifted his eyes, stepped down from the verandah, and went up to Missy.

"Missy," said he, in a low, hoarse voice, "Missy, I'll take your word as soon as the word of a person I've never set eyes on before. Is this true, or is it not? Are you, or are you not, Miriam Oliver, the daughter of my old friend?"

"It is true," said Missy. "I'm no more Miriam Oliver than you are."

Neither question nor answer had reached the ears of those in the verandah. But they saw David turn towards them with his head hanging lower than before, and he tottered as he rejoined them. Miss Oliver, however, may have guessed what had passed, for she smiled a supercilious smile which no one happened to observe. This young lady was a contrast to her impersonator in every imaginable way. She was not nearly so tall, and she had exceedingly fair hair. Her nose was tip-tilted to begin with, but she seemed to have a habit of turning it up even beyond the design of nature. This was perhaps justified on the present occasion. She was very fashionably dressed in a costume of extremely light gray; and in the dilapidated framework of the old verandah she was by far the most incongruous figure upon the scene.

"Has she anything to say for herself?" Mrs. Teesdale demanded of her husband. He shook his head despondently.

And then, at last, Missy opened her mouth.

"I have only this to say for myself. It isn't much, but Mr. Teesdale will tell you that it's the truth. It's only that I did do my level best to make a clean breast to him last night."

"She did!" exclaimed the old man, after a moment's rapid consideration. "Now I see what she meant. To think that I never saw then!"

"You were very dense," said Missy; "but not worse than John William. I did my best to tell you last night, and I did my best to tell him only this morning, but neither of you would understand."

As she spoke to the old man her voice was strangely gentle, and a smile was hovering about the corners of her mouth when she ceased. Moreover, her words had brought out a faint ray of light upon Mr. Teesdale's dejected mien.

"It's a fact!" he cried, turning to the others. "She did her best to confess last night. She did confess. I remember all about it now. It was a full confession, if only I'd put two and two together. But—well, I never could have believed it of her. That was it!"

He finished on a sufficiently reproachful note.

Nevertheless, Mrs. Teesdale turned upon him as fiercely as though he had spoken from a brief in Missy's defence.

"What if she had confessed? I'm ashamed of you, David, going on as though that could ha' made any difference! She'd still have deceived us and lied to us all these weeks. Black is black and this—this woman—is that black that God Himself couldn't whiten her!"

And Mrs. Teesdale shook her fist at the guilty girl.

"We have none of us a right to say that," murmured David.

"But I do say it, and I mean it, too. I say that she'd still have stolen Miriam's letter of introduction, and come here deliberately and passed herself off as Miriam, and slept under our roof, and eaten-our bread, under false pretences—false pretences as shall put her in prison if I have anything to do with it! No confession could have undone all that; and no confession shall keep her out of prison neither, not if I know it!"

Some of them were expecting Missy to take to her heels any moment; but she never showed the least sign of doing so.

"No, nothing can undo it," she said herself. "I've known that for some time, and I shan't be sorry to pay the cost."

Then the real Miss Oliver put in her word. It was winged with a sneer.

"It was hardly a compliment," she said, "to take her for me! You might ask her, by the way, when and where she stole my letters. I lost several." She could not permit herself to address the culprit direct.

"I'll tell you that," said Missy, "and everything else too, if you like to listen."

"Do, Missy!" cried Arabella, speaking also for the first time. "And then I'll tell them something."

"Be sharp, then," said Mrs. Teesdale. "We're not going to stand here much longer listening to the likes of you. If you've got much to say, you'd better keep it for the magistrate!"

Missy shook her head at Arabella, stared briefly but boldly at Mrs. Teesdale, and then addressed herself to the fair girl in gray, who raised her eyebrows at the liberty.

"You remember the morning after you landed in the Parramatta? It was a very hot day, about a couple of months ago, but in the forenoon you went for a walk with a lady friend. And you took the Fitzroy Gardens on your way."

Miss Oliver nodded, without thinking whom she was nodding to. This was because she had become very much interested all in a moment; the next, she regretted that nod, and set herself to listen with a fixed expression of disgust.

"You walked through the Fitzroy Gardens, you stopped to look at all the statues, and then you sat down on a seat. I saw you, because I was sitting on the next seat. You sat on that seat, and you took out some letters and read bits of them to your friend. I could hear your voices, but I couldn't hear what you were saying, and I didn't want to, either. I had my own things to think about, and they weren't very nice thinking, I can tell you! That hot morning, I remember, I was just wishing and praying to get out of Melbourne for good and all. And when I passed your seat after you'd left it, there were your letters lying under it on the gravel. I picked them up, and I looked up and down for you and your friend. You were out of sight, but I made for the entrance and waited for you there. Yes, I did—you may sneer as much as you like! But you never came, and when I went back to my lodgings I took your letters with me."

Still the young lady sneered without speaking, and Missy hardened her heart.

"I read them every one," she said defiantly. "I had nothing to do with myself during the day, and very good reading they were! And in the afternoon, just for the lark of it, I took your letter of introduction, which was among the rest, and then I took the 'bus and came out here."

She turned now to David, and continued in that softer voice which she could not help when speaking to him.

"It was only for the fun of it! I had no idea of ever coming out again. But you made so much of me; you were all so kind—and the place—it was heaven to a girl like me!"

Here she surprised them all, but one, by breaking down. Mr. Teesdale was not astonished. When she recovered her self-control it was to him she turned her swimming eyes; it was the look in his that enabled her to go on.

"If you knew what my life was!" she wailed; "if you knew how I hated it! If you knew how I longed to come out into the country, when I saw what the country was like! I had never seen your Australian country before. It was all new to me. I had only been a year out from home, but at home I lived all my life in London. My God, what a life! But I never meant to come back to you—I said I wouldn't—and then

I said you must take the consequences if I did. Even when I said good-bye to you, Mr. Teesdale, I never really thought of coming back; so you see I repaid your kindness not only by lies, but by robbing you—"

She pulled herself up. David had glanced uneasily towards his wife. The girl understood.

"By robbing you of your peace of mind, for I said that I would come back, never meaning to at all. And now do you know why I was in such a hurry to get to the theatre? Yes, it was because I had an engagement there. All the rest was lies. And I never should have come out to you again, only at last I saw in the Argus that she—that Miss Oliver—had gone to Sydney. Don't you remember how you'd seen it too? Well, then I felt safe. I was only a ballet-girl, I'd done better once, for at home I'd had a try in the halls. So I chucked it up and came out to you. I thought I should see in the Argus when Miss Oliver came back from Sydney, but somehow I've missed it. And now—"

She flung wide her arms, and raised her eyes, and looked from the sky overhead to the river-timber away down to the right, and from the river-timber to David Teesdale.

"And now you may put me in prison as fast as you like. I've been here two months. They're well worth twelve of hard labour, these last two months on this farm!"

She had finished.

Mrs. Teesdale turned to her husband. "The brazen slut!" she cried. "Not a word of penitence! She doesn't care—not she! To prison she shall go, and we'll see whether that makes her care."

But David shook his head. "No, no, my dear! I will not have her sent to prison. What good could it do us or her? Rather let her go away quietly, and may the Almighty forgive her—and—and make her—"

He looked down, and there was Missy on her knees to him. "Can you forgive me?" she cried passionately. "Say that you forgive me, and then send me to prison or any place you like. Only say that you forgive me if you can."

"I can," said the old man softly, "and I do. But I am not the One. You shall not go to prison, but you must go away from us, and may God have mercy on you and help you to lead a better life hereafter. You—you have been very kind to me in little ways, Missy, and I shall try to think kindly of you too."

He spoke with great emotion, and as he did so his trembling hand rested ever so lightly upon the red head from which the hat was tilted back. And the girl seized that kind, caressing hand, and raised it to her lips, but let it drop without allowing them to touch it. Then she rose and retreated under their eyes. And all the good women had been awed to silence by this leave-taking; but one of them recovered herself in time to put a shot into the retiring enemy.

"Mr. Teesdale is a deal too lenient," cried the farmer's wife. "He's been like that all his life! If I'd had my way, to prison you should have gone—to prison you should have gone, you shameless bad woman, you!"

Old David heard it without a word. He was seeing the last of Missy as she descended the pad-dock by the path that led down to the slip-rails; the very last that he saw of her was the sunlight upon her hair and hat.

Arabella had darted into the house, and she now came out with a small bundle of things in her arms. With these she followed Missy, coming up with her at the slip-rails, against which she was leaning with her face buried in her hands.

Now this was the spot where Arabella had first met the man from whom this abandoned girl had rescued her, body and soul. She had desired to tell them all that story, to show them the good in Missy, and so make them less hard upon her. The person who had prevented her, by forbidding look and vigorous gesture, was Missy herself....

It was half an hour later when Arabella returned to the house. This was what she was in time to see and hear.

The real Miss Oliver was sitting in the buggy beside the man in livery, replying, with chilly smiles and decided shakes of her fair head, to the joint remonstrances, exhortations, and persuasions of Mr. and Mrs. Teesdale, who were standing together on the near side of the buggy.

"But I've just made the tea this minute," Arabella heard her mother complain. "Surely you'll stop and have your tea with us after coming all this way?"

"Thank you so much; it is very kind of you; but I promised to be back at the picnic in time for tea, and it is some miles away."

"But Mrs. Teesdale takes a special pride in her tea," said David, "and she has made it, so that we shouldn't keep you waiting at all."

"So kind of you; but I'm afraid I have stayed too long already. I was just waiting to say goodbye to Mrs. Teesdale. Good-bye again—"

"Come, Miriam," said Mrs. T., a little testily, "or we shall be offended!"

"I should be very sorry to offend you, I am sure, but really my friends lent me their buggy on the express condition—"

From her manner Mr. Teesdale saw that further pressing would be useless.

"We will let you go now," said he, "if you will come back and stay with us as long as you can."

"For a month at least," added Mrs. T.

Miss Oliver looked askance.

"We are such very old friends of your parents," pleaded David.

"We would like to be your parents as long as you remain in Australia," Mrs. Teesdale went so far as to say. And already her tone was genuinely kind and motherly, as it had never become towards poor Missy in all the past two months.

Miss Oliver raised her eyebrows; luckily they were so light that the grimace was less noticeable than it otherwise might have been.

"Suppose we write about it?" said she at length. "Yes, that would be the best. I have several engagements, and I am only staying out a few weeks longer. But I will certainly come out and see you again if I can."

"And stay with us?" said Mrs. T.

"And stay a night with you—if I can."

"By this time," exclaimed David, "we might have had our tea and been done with it. Won't you think better of it and jump down now? Come, for your parents' sakes—I wish you would."

"So do I, dear knows!" said Mrs. Teesdale wistfully. But Miss Oliver, this time without speaking, shook her head more decidedly than ever; gave the old people a bow apiece worthy of Hyde Park; and drove off without troubling to notice the daughter of the house, who, however, was not thinking of her at all, but of Missy.

CHAPTER XVI

A MAN' RESOLVE

How to tell John William when he came home, that was the prime difficulty in the mind of Arabella. Tell him she must, as soon as ever he got in. She felt it of importance that he should hear the news first from herself, and not, for example, from their mother. But it was going to be a very disagreeable duty; more so, indeed, than she ever could have dreamt, until Missy herself warned her, almost with her last words, at the slip-rails. Missy had opened her eyes for her during those few final minutes. Till then she had suspected nothing between her brother and the girl. And now the case seemed so clear and so inevitable that her chief cause for wonderment lay in her own previous want of perception. It made her very nervous, however, with the news still to break to John William. She wished that he would make haste home. He had ridden off early in the afternoon to look up another young farmer several miles distant; not that he wanted to see anyone at all, but because he was ill at ease and anxious to be out of Missy's way, as Arabella now made sure. But poor Missy! And poor John William! Would they ever see each other again? She hoped not. Her heart grieved for them both, but she hoped not. No woman, being also a sister of the man concerned, could know about another woman what Arabella now knew against Missy, and hope otherwise. And the state of her own feelings in the matter was her uppermost trouble, when at last John William trotted his mare into the yard, and Arabella followed him into the stable.

Then and there she hurriedly told all. Her great dread was that their mother might appear on the scene and tell it in her way. But the attitude of the man greatly astonished Arabella. He took the news so coolly—but that was not it. He seemed not at all agitated to hear what Missy was, and who she was not, but very much so on learning how summarily she had been sent about her business. He said very little even then, but Arabella knew that he was trembling all over as he unsaddled the mare.

"My heart bled for the poor thing," she added, speaking the simple truth. "It would have bled even if she hadn't done more for me than ever I can tell anybody. I was thankful I went after her, and saw the last of her at the rails—"

"Which way did she go?"

"To the township to begin with; but she gave me—"

"Which way did she mean to go—straight back to Melbourne?"

"She didn't say. I was going on to tell you that at the slip-rails she gave me some messages for you, John William."

"We will have them afterwards. Let us go in to supper now."

"Very well—but stay! Are you prepared for mother? She is dreadful about it; she makes it even worse than it is."

"I am prepared for anything. I shall not open my mouth."

Nor did he; but the provocation was severe. Mrs. Teesdale was glad of an opportunity of rehearsing the whole story from beginning to end. This enabled her to decide what epithets were too weak for the occasion, and what names were as nearly bad enough for Missy as any that a respectable woman could lay her tongue to; also, by what she now said, this excellent woman strengthened her own rather recent convictions that she had "suspected something of the kind" about Missy from the very first. Certainly she had felt a strong antipathetic instinct from the very first. Quite as certainly she had now just cause for righteous rage and desires the most vindictive. Yet there was not one of those three, her nearest, who did not feel a fresh spasm of pain at each violent word, because every one of them, save the wife and mother, had some secret cause to think softly of the godless girl who was gone, and to look back upon her more in pity than in blame.

For sadness, Mr. Teesdale was the saddest of them all. He crept to his bed a shaken old man, and had to listen to his wife until he thought she must break his heart. Meantime Arabella and John William foregathered in the latter's room, and talked in whispers in order not to wake two old people who had neither of them closed an eye.

"About those messages," said John William. "What were they?"

He was sitting on the edge of his bed, and he pared a cake of tobacco as he spoke. His wideawake lay on the quilt beside him, and he had not taken off his boots. Arabella stood uneasily.

"Poor girl! she spoke about you a good deal just at the last."

Arabella hesitated.

"I want to know what she said," observed John William dryly.

"Well, first she was sorry you weren't there."

"If I had been she never should have gone like that!"

"What, not when everything had come out—"

"No, not at all; she shouldn't have been kicked out, anyway. I'd have given her time and then driven her back to Melbourne, with all her things. What right have we with them, I should like to know?"

"She wanted us to keep them, she—"

"Wanted us! I'd have let her want, if I'd been here. However, go on. She was sorry I wasn't there, was she?"

"Well, at first she said so, but in a little while she told me that she was glad. And after that she said I didn't know how glad she was for you never to set eyes on her again!"

"Never's a long time," muttered John William.

"Did she explain herself?" he added, as loud as they ventured to speak.

"Y—yes." Arabella was hesitating.

"Then out with it!"

"She told me—it can't be true, but yet she did tell me—that you—fancied yourself in love with her, John William!"

"It isn't true."

"Thank God for that!"

"Stop a moment. Not so fast, my girl! It isn't true—because there's no fancy at all about it, d'ye see?"

Arabella saw. It was written and painted all over his lined yet glowing face; but where there could be least mistake about it was in his eyes. They were ablaze with love—with love for a woman who had neither name, honour, nor common purity. He could not know this. But Arabella knew all, and it was her business—nay, her solemn undertaking—to repeat all that she knew to John William.

"I was told," she faltered, "what to say to you if you said that."

"Who told you?"

"She did—Missy."

"Then say it right out."

But that was difficult between brother and sister. At first he refused to understand, and then he refused to believe.

"It's a lie!" he cried hoarsely. "I don't believe a word of it!"

"And do you suppose I would make it up? Upon my sacred honour, John William, it is only what she told me with her own—"

"I know that; it's her lie—I never meant it was yours. No, no, it's Missy's lie to choke me off. But it shan't! No, by Heaven, and it shouldn't if it were the living truth!"

There was no more to be said. The man knew that, and he relit the pipe, which he had scarcely tasted, without looking at the sister whom he had silenced. Presently he said in a perfectly passionless voice, coming back from the unspeakable to a point which it was possible to discuss:

"About those things of hers—all her clothes. Did you say that she wanted us to keep them? And if so, why?"

"Because," said Arabella with some reluctance, "they were bought with money which—as she said herself—she had obtained from father on false pretences."

It may have been because he was now quite calm outwardly, but at this the man winced more visibly than at what had come out before.

"From father," he repeated at length; "he couldn't let her have much, anyway!"

"He let her have twenty pounds."

"Never; the bank wouldn't let him have it."

"The bank didn't; he got it on his watch."

"On the watch that's—mending?"

The truth flashed across him before the words were out. Arabella nodded her head, and her brother bowed his in trouble.

"Yes, that's bad," said he, as though nothing else had been. "There's no denying it, that is bad." It was a thing he could realise; that was why he took it thus disproportionately to heart.

"Surely it is all bad together!" said Arabella. John William spent some minutes in a study of the bare boards by his bedside.

"Where do you think she went to?" he said at last, looking up.

"I have no idea."

"Have you told me all that she said? She didn't—she didn't send any other messages?" It was wistfully asked.

"No, none; but she did tell me how she hopes and prays that you will never give her another thought. She declares she has never given a single thought to you. It is true, too, I am sure."

"We shall see—we shall see. So you have no idea where she went? She gave you no hint of any sort or kind?"

"None whatever."

"She has gone back to Melbourne, think you?"

"I don't know where else she could go to."

"No more do I," said John William, rising from the bed at last. He opened the window softly and looked out into the night. "No more do I see where else she could go to," he whispered over again. Then he turned round to Arabella. She was watching him closely. Neither of them spoke. But John William picked his wideawake from off the bed and jammed it over his brows. Then he took a pair of spurs from the drawers-head and dropped them into his coat pocket. Then he faced Arabella afresh.

"Do you know what I am going to do?"

"I can guess. You are going to ride into Melbourne and look for Missy."

"I am—and now, at once. I'm going out by that window. Don't shut it, because I shall be back before milking, and shall come in the same way I get out."

"But you'll never see her, John William; you'll never see her," said Arabella in misery. "It'll be like hunting for a needle in a haystack!"

"You may always find the needle—there is always a chance. For me, if half of what she told you has a word of truth in it I shall have a better chance by night than by day. It can't be much after eleven now, and I guess I shall do it to-night in half an hour."

"But if you don't see her?"

"Then I shall have another try to-morrow night—and another the next—and another the night after that. There are plenty of horses in the paddock; there are some that haven't been ridden this long time, and some that nobody can ride but me. The mare will have to sweat for it to-night, but not after to-night. Only look here. I shall be found out sooner or later, then there will be a row, and you know who'll make it. You'll let it be later, won't you,'.ella, so far as you're concerned?"

"You must know that I will!"

"Then bless you, my dear, and good night."

They had seldom kissed since they were little children. They were both of them over thirty now, in respect of mere years. But with his beard tickling the woman's cheek, the man whispered, "You said that she had done something for you, too, you know!"

And the woman answered, "Something more than I can ever tell any of you. You little know what I might have come to, but for Missy. Yet what are you to do with her, poor Jack, if you do find her?"

And the man said, "Make her good again, so help me God!"

CHAPTER XVII

THE TWO MIRIAMS.

A Sunday morning early in the following February; in fact, the first Sunday of the month.

It was, perhaps, the freshest and coolest morning of any kind that the hot young year had as yet brought forth. Nevertheless, neither Mr. nor Mrs. Teesdale had gone to chapel, as was their wont. For this Sabbath day was also one requiring a red letter in the calendar of the Teesdales, insomuch as it was the solitary entire day which a greatly honoured visitor over the week-end had consented, after much ill-bred importuning, to give to her father's old friends at the farm.

The visitor was gone to chapel with Arabella. But the farmer and his wife had stayed at home, the one to shoot a hare, and the other to cook it for the very special Sunday dinner which the occasion demanded.

Naturally David's part was soon performed, because the old man was so good a shot still, and there were plenty of hares about the place. It was less natural in one of his serene disposition to light a pipe afterwards and sit down in the verandah expressly and deliberately to think of things which could only trouble him. This, however, was what he proceeded to do. And the things troubled him more and more the longer he allowed his mind to dwell upon them.

One thing was the whole miserable episode of Missy, of whom the old man could not possibly help thinking, in that verandah.

Another was the manner and bearing of the proper Miriam, which was of the kind to make simple homely folks feel small and awkward.

A third thing was the difference between the two Miriams.

"She is not like her mother, and she certainly is not like her father—not as I knew him," muttered David with reference to the real one. "But she's exactly like her portrait in yon group. Put her in the sun, and you see it in a minute. She frowns just like that still. She has much the same expression whenever she isn't speaking to you or you aren't speaking to her. It isn't a kind expression, and I wish I never saw it. I wish it was more like—"

He ceased thinking so smoothly, for as a stone stars a pane of glass, that had shot into his mind's eye which made cross-roads of his thoughts. He took one of the roads and sat pulling at his pipe. Here from the verandah there was no view to be had of the river-timber and the distant ranges so beloved of the old man's gaze. But his eyes wandered down the paddock in front of the farmhouse, and thence to the township roofs, shifting from one to another of such as shone salient in the morning sun, and finally running up the parched and yellow hill upon the farther side. That way lay Melbourne, nine or ten miles to the south. And on this hill-top, between withered grass and dark blue sky, the old eyes rested; and the old lips kept clouding with tobacco-smoke the bit of striking sky-line, for the satisfaction of seeing it break through the cloud next instant; while on the worn face the passing flicker of a smile only showed the shadow of pain that was there all the time, until at length no more smoke came to soften the garish brilliance of the southern sky.

Then David lowered his eyes and knocked the ashes out of his pipe. And presently he sighed a few syllables aloud:

"Ay, Missy! Poor thing! Poor girl!"

For on the top of that hill, between grass and sky, between puff and puff from his own pipe, a mammoth Missy had appeared in a vision to David Teesdale. Nor was it one Missy, but a whole set of her in a perfect sequence of visions. And this sort of thing was happening to the old man every day.

There was some reason for it. With all her badness the girl had certainly shown David personally a number of small attentions such as he had never experienced at any hands but hers. She had filled his pipe, and fetched his slippers, and taken his arm whenever they chanced to be side by side for half a dozen steps. His own daughter never dreamt of such things, unless asked to do them, which was rare. But Missy had done them continually and of her own accord. She had taken it into her own head to read to the old man every day; she had listened to anything and all things he had to say to her, as Arabella had never listened in her life. Not that the daughter was at all uncommon in this respect; the wife was just the same. The real Miriam, too, showed plainly enough to a sensitive eye that poor David's conversation interested her not in the least. So it was only Missy who was uncommon—in caring for anything that he had to say. And this led Mr. Teesdale to remember the little good in her, and doubtless to exaggerate it, without thinking of the enormous evil; even so that when he did remember everything the old man, for one, was still unable to think of the impostor without a certain lingering tenderness.

There kept continually recurring to him things that she had said, her way of saying them, the tones of her voice, the complete look and sound of her in sundry little scenes that had actually taken place during her stay at the farm. Two such had been played all over again between the smoke of his pipe, the rim of yellow grass, and the background of blue sky which had formed the theatre of his thoughts. One of the two was the occasion of Missy's first blood-shedding with John William's gun. David recalled her sudden coming round the corner of the house—this corner. A whirlwind in a white dress, the flush of haste upon her face, the light of triumph in her eyes, the trail of the wind about her disorderly red hair. So had she come to him and thrown her victim at his feet as he sat where he was sitting now. And in a trice he had taken the triumph out of her by telling her what it was that she had shot, and why she ought not to have shot it at all. He could still see the look in her face as she gazed at her dead handiwork in the light of those candid remarks: first it was merely crestfallen, then it was ashamed, as her excitement subsided and she realised that she had done a cruel thing at best. She was not naturally cruel—a thousand trifles had proved her to be the very reverse. Her heart might be black by reason of her life, but by nature it was soft and kind. Kindness was something! It made up for some things, too.

Thus David would console himself, fetching his consolation from as far as you please. But even he could extract scant comfort from the other little incident which had come into his head. This was when Missy drank off Old Willie's whisky without the flicker of an eyelid; there has hitherto been no occasion to mention the matter, which was not more startling than many others which happened about the same time. Suffice it now to explain that Mr. Teesdale was in the habit of mixing every evening, and setting in safety on the kitchen mantelpiece, a pannikin of grog for Old Willie, who started townwards with the milk at two o'clock every morning. One fine evening Missy happened to see David prepare this potion, and asked what it was, getting as answer, "Old Willie's medicine;" whereupon the girl took it up, smelt it, and drank it off before the horrified old gentleman had time to interfere. "It's whisky!" he gasped. "Good whisky, too," replied Missy, smacking her lips. "But it was a stiff dose—I make it stiff so as to keep Old Willie from wanting any at the other end. You'd better be off to bed, Missy, before it makes you feel queer."

"Queer!" cried Missy. "One tot like that! Do you suppose I've never tasted whisky before?" And indeed she behaved a little better than usual during the remainder of the evening.

That alone should have aroused his suspicions—so David felt now. But at the time he had told nobody a word about the trick, and had passed it over in his own mind as one of the many "habits and ways which were not the habits and ways of young girls in our day." Their name had indeed been legion as applied to the perjured pretender; that sentence in Mr. Oliver's letter, like the remark about "modern mannerisms," was fatally appropriate to her. Remained the question, how could those premonitory touches apply to a young lady so cultivated and so superior as the real Miriam Oliver?

It was a question which Mr. Teesdale found very difficult to answer; it was a question which was driven to the back of his brain, for the time being, by the return of the superior young lady herself, with Arabella, from the township chapel.

David jumped up and hurried out to meet them. Miss Oliver wore a look which he could not read, because it was the look of boredom, with which David was not familiar. He thought she was tired, and offered her his arm. She refused it with politeness and a perfunctory smile.

"I'm afraid you've had a very hot walk," said the old man. "Who preached, Arabella?"

"Mr. Appleton. Miss Oliver didn't think—"

"Ah! I thought he would!" cried David with enthusiasm. "We're very proud of Mr. Appleton's sermons. It will be interesting to hear how he strikes a young lady—"

"She didn't think much of him," Arabella went on to state with impersonal candour.

"Nay, come!" And Mr. Teesdale looked for contradiction to the young lady herself; but though the latter raised her eyebrows at Arabella's way of putting it, she did not mince matters in the least. Perhaps this was one of those ways or habits.

"It was better than I expected," she said, with a small and languid smile.

"But didn't you like our minister, Miss Oliver? We all think so highly of him."

"Oh, I am sure he is an excellent man, and what he said seemed extremely well meant; but one has heard all that before, over and over again, and rather better put."

"Ah, at Home, no doubt. Yes; I suppose you would now, in London. However," added David, throwing up his chin in an attempt to look less snubbed than he felt as they came into the verandah, "as long as you don't regret having gone! That's the main thing—not the sermon. The prayers and the worship are of much more account, and I knew you'd enjoy them. Take this chair, Miss Oliver, and get cooled a bit before you go inside."

Miss Oliver stopped short of saying what she thought of the prayers, which, indeed, had been mostly extemporised by the Rev. Mr. Appleton. But Arabella, had she not gone straight into the house, would have had something to say on this point, for Miss Oliver had been excessively frank with her on the way home, and she was nettled. It was odd how none of them save Mrs. Teesdale (who was not sensitive) thought of calling the real Miriam by her Christian name. That young lady had refused the chair, but she stood for a moment taking off her gloves.

"And why didn't you come to chapel, Mr. Teesdale?" she asked, for something to say, simply.

"Aha!" said David slyly. "That's tellings. I make a rule of going, and it's a rule I very seldom break; but I'm afraid I broke it this morning—ay, and the Sabbath itself—I've broken that and all!"

Miss Miriam was a little too visibly unamused, because, with all her culture, she had omitted to cultivate the kind art of appreciation. She had never studied the gentle trick of keeping one's companions on good terms with themselves, and it did not come natural to her. So David was made to feel that he had said something foolish, and this led him into an unnecessary explanation.

"You see, in this country, in the hot weather, meat goes bad before you know where you are." This put up the backs of Miss Oliver's eyebrows to begin with.

"You can't keep a thing a day, so, if I must tell you, I've been shooting a hare for our dinners. Mrs. T. is busy cooking it now. You see, if we'd hung it up even for a couple of hours—"

"Please don't go into particulars," cried Miss Oliver, with a terrible face and much asperity of tone. "There was no need for you to tell me at all. You dine late, then, on Sundays?"

"No, early, just as usual; it will be ready by the time you've got your things off."

"What—the hare that you've only shot since we went out?"

"Why, to be sure."

Miss Oliver went in to take off her things without another word. And David gathered from his guilty conscience that he had said what he had no call to say, what it was bad taste to say, what nobody but a very ill-bred old man would have dreamt of saying; but presently he knew it to his cost.

For nothing would induce the visitor to touch that hare, though Mrs. Teesdale had cooked it with her own hands. She had to say so herself, but Miss Miriam steadily shook her head; nor did there appear to be much use in pressing her. Mrs. Teesdale only made matters worse by so doing. But it is impossible not to sympathise with Mrs. Teesdale. She was by no means so strong a woman as her manifold and varied exertions would have led one to suppose. A hot two hours in the kitchen had left their mark upon her, and being tired at all events, if not in secret bodily pain, she very quickly became angry also. There was, in fact, every prospect of a scene, when David interposed and took the entire blame for having divulged to Miss Oliver the all too modern history of the hare. Then Mrs. Teesdale was angry, but only with her husband. With Miriam she proceeded to sympathise from that instant; indeed, she had set herself to make much of this Miriam from the first; and the matter ended by the young lady at last overcoming her scruples and condescending to one minute slice from the middle of the back. But she had worn throughout these regrettable proceedings a smile, hardly noticeable in itself, but of peculiarly exasperating qualities, if one did happen to remark it. And it had not escaped John William, who sat at the table without speaking a word, feeling, in any case, disinclined to open his mouth before so superior a being as this young lady from England.

In the heat of the afternoon, however, the younger Teesdale found the elder in the parlour, alone too, but walking up and down, as if ill at ease; and John William then had his say.

"Where's everybody?" he asked, putting his head into the room first of all. Then he entered bodily and shut the door behind him. "Where's our precious guest?" he cried, in no promising tone.

"She's gone to lie down, and so has—"

"That's all right! I shan't be sorry myself if she goes on lying down for the rest of the day. I don't know what you think of her, father, but I do know what I think!"

Mr. Teesdale continued to pace the floor with bent body and badly troubled face, but he said nothing.

"She's what I told you she would be," proceeded the son, "in the very beginning. I told you she'd be stuck up—and good Lord, isn't she? I said we didn't want that kind here, and no more we do. No, I'm dashed if we do! Don't you remember? It was the time you read us the old man's letter. I liked the letter and I might like the old man, but I'm dashed if I like his daughter! She doesn't take after her father, I'll be bound."

"Not unless he is very much changed," admitted David sadly. "Still, I think you are rather hard upon her, John William."

"Hard upon her! Haven't I been watching her? Haven't I ears and eyes in my head, like everybody else? It's only one meal I've set down to beside her, so far, but one 'll do for me! With her nasty supercilious smile, and her no-thank-you this and no-thank-you that! I never did know anybody take such a delight in refusing things. Look at her about that hare!"

"Yes; and your mother had spent all morning at it. I'm very much afraid she's knocked herself up over it, for she's lying down, too. Your mother is not so strong as she was, John William. I'm very much afraid that matter of Missy has been preying on her nerves."

"I'd rather have Missy than this here Miriam," said John William, after a pause, and all at once his voice was full of weariness.

The same thought was in Mr. Teesdale's mind, but he did not give expression to it. Presently he said, still pacing the room with his long-legged, weak-kneed stride:

"I wonder what Mr. Oliver meant when he hinted that I should find Miriam so different from the girls of our day? Where are the tricks and habits that he alluded to? Poor Missy had plenty, but I can't see any in Miriam."

"Can't you? Then I can. Ways of another kind altogether. Did the girls in your day turn up their noses at things before people's faces?"

"No."

"Did they sneer when they talked to their elders and betters?"

"No; but we are only Miriam's elders, mind—not her betters."

"Could they smile without looking supercilious, and could they open their mouths without showing their superiority?"

"Of course they could."

"There you are then! One more question—about Mr. Oliver this time. When you left the old country he hadn't the position he has now, had he?"

"No, no; very far from it. He was just beginning business, and in a small way, too. Now he is a very wealthy man."

"Then he hadn't got as good an education as he's been able to give his children, I reckon?"

"No, you're right. We went to school together, he and I," said Mr. Teesdale simply.

"Then don't you see?" cried his son, jumping up from the sofa where he had been sitting, while the old man still walked up and down the room. "Don't you see, father? Mr. Oliver was warning you against what he himself had suffered from. You bet that Miss Miriam picks him up, and snubs him and sneers at him, just as she does with us!"

Which was the cleverest deduction that this unsophisticated young farmer had ever arrived at in his life; but puzzling constantly over another matter had lent a new activity to his brain, and much worry had sharpened his wits.

Old Teesdale accepted his son's theory readily enough, but yet sorrowfully, and the more so because the more he saw of his old friend's child, the less he liked her.

Indeed, she was not at all an agreeable young person. It appeared that she had been merely reading in her own room, so when Arabella owned to having been asleep in hers, she looked duly and consciously superior. There was something comic about that look of conscious superiority which broke out upon this young lady's face upon the least provocation, but it is difficult to give an impression of it in words—it was so slight, and yet so plain. To be sure, she was the social as well as the intellectual superior of the simple folk at the farm, but that in itself was not so very much to be proud of, and at any rate one would not have expected a tolerably well-educated girl to exhale superiority with every breath. But this was the special weakness of Miss Miriam Oliver. Even the fact that some of the Teesdales read the Family Cherub was an opportunity which she could not resist. She took up a number and satirised the Family Cherub most unmercifully. Then she was queer about the poor old piano in the best parlour. She played a few bars upon it—she could play very well—and then jumped up shuddering. Certainly the piano was terribly out of tune; but not more so than this young Englishwoman's manners. In conversation with the Teesdales there was only one subject that really interested her.

It was a subject which had been fully dealt with at supper on the Saturday night, when Mrs. Teesdale had waxed very warm thereon. Old Teesdale and Arabella had listened in silence because to them it was not quite such a genial topic. John William had not been there; the misfortune was that he did sit down to the Sunday supper, when Miss Oliver brought up this subject again.

"Did my under-study like cocoa, then?" she inquired, having herself refused to take any, much to Mrs. T.'. discomfiture.

"You mean that impudent baggage?" said the latter. "Ay, she was the opposite extreme to you, Miriam. She took all she could get, you may be sure! She made the best use of her time!"

"Do tell me some more about her," said Miss Oliver. "It is most interesting."

"Nay, I would rather not speak of her," replied Mrs. Teesdale, who was only too delighted to do so when sure of a sympathetic hearing. "It was the most impudent piece of wickedness that ever I heard tell of in my life."

"The queer thing to me," remarked Miss Oliver, "is that you ever should have believed her. Fancy taking such a creature for me! It was scarcely a compliment, Mrs. Teesdale. A more utterly vulgar person one could hardly wish to see."

"My dear," began Mr. Teesdale nervously, "she behaved very badly, we know; yet she had her good points—"

"Hold your tongue, David!" cried his wife, whom nothing incensed more than a good word for Missy. "She curry-favoured with you, so you try to whitewash her. I wonder what Miriam will think of you? However, Miriam, I can tell you that I never believed in her—never once! A brazen, shameless, lying, thieving hussy, that's what she—"

A heavy fist had banged the table at the lower end, so that every cup danced in its saucer, and all eyes were turned upon John William, who sat in his place—trembling a little—very pale—but with eyes that glared alarmingly, first at his mother, then at the guest.

"What did she steal?" he thundered out. "You may be ashamed of yourself, mother, trying to make the girl out worse than she was. And you, Miss Oliver—I wonder you couldn't find something better to talk about—something in better taste!"

Miss Oliver put up her pale eyebrows.

"This is interesting!" she exclaimed. "To think that one should come here to learn what is, and what is not good taste! Perhaps you preferred my—my predecessor to me, Mr. Teesdale?"

"I did so!" said John William stoutly.

"Ah, I thought as much. She was, of course, rather more in your line."

"By the Lord," answered the young man, forgetting himself entirely, "if you were more in hers it would be the better for them that have to do with you. She could have taught you common civility, at any rate, and common kindness, and two or three other common things that you seem never to have been taught in your life!" There was a moment's complete silence. Then Miss Oliver got steadily to her feet.

"After that," she said to David, "I think my room is the best place for me—and the safest too."

She proceeded to the door without let or hindrance. All save herself were too much startled to speak or to act. Mr. Teesdale was gazing through the gun-room window with a weary face; his wife held her side as if it were a physical trouble with her; while Arabella looked in terror at John William, who was staring unflinchingly at the first woman he had lived to insult. The latter had reached the threshold, where, however, she turned to leave them something to keep.

"It serves me right," she said. "I might have known what to expect if I came here."

CHAPTER XVIII

THE WAY OF ALL FLESH

Ay, it's been a bad job," said David. "But it's over and done with now—that's one thing."

He meant the whole matter, from Mr. Oliver's letter about Miriam to this young lady's ultimate depressing visit; but in his heart he was thinking more of things and a person that came in between; and he glanced in wonder at his wife, who for once had missed an opening to loosen her lips and rail at that person and those things.

They were driving into Melbourne, the old couple together, and such a thing was rare. Moreover, the proposal had been Mrs. Teesdale's, which was rarer still. But rarest of all was her reason, namely, that there were several little odds and ends which she wanted to buy for herself. They had been married thirty-five years, but she had never been known deliberately to buy herself any odds or ends before.

"Fallals?" said David chuckling.

"No such thing; you know nothing about it, David."

"Ribbons?"

"Rubbish," said Mrs. Teesdale; and David looked at her again, for there was no edge on the word, and, after thirty-five years, there was a something in the woman which was new and puzzling to the man.

What was it? A week and more had passed since Miriam Oliver left them, with undisguised relief in her eyes and the coldest of cold farewells upon her lips, which not even Mrs. Teesdale, who half attempted it, was allowed to kiss in memory of her parents. Since that day Mrs. T. had not been herself; but David was only now beginning to perceive it. When one has lived thirty-five years with another the master-spirit of the pair, it must be hard indeed for the weaker to discern the first false ring, telling of the first flaw in the stronger vessel. And the weaker vessel need not necessarily be the woman, that is the worst of it; in the Teesdales' case it was certainly plain enough which, was which. So the feeble and indolent old man was slow to see infirmity in the active, energetic body, his wife; indeed, the infirmity did not show itself as such quite immediately. It came out first of all in snapping and storming, in continual irritation, culminating in furies as insane as the rage of babes and sucklings. In this stage she would take and tear the unforgotten Missy into little pieces when other irritating matter chanced to flag; and once boxed Arabella's ears for daring to hint that the ways of the genuine Miriam were themselves not absolutely perfect. The name of Missy, whom she could not abuse too roundly, had the excellent effect upon her of taking off the steam; that of Miriam caused certain explosion, because for her Mrs. Teesdale would stick up with her lips while resenting most bitterly in her secret heart every remembered word and look of this young lady. The memory of both girls was gall and wormwood to her. There was only this difference, that she lost her temper in defending Miriam, and found it again in reviling Missy. But now, after not many days, that temper was much less readily lost and found; the sharpness was gone from the tongue to the face; all at once the woman was grown old; and he who had aged before her, though by her side, was the last to realise that she had caught him up.

She could milk no longer. One afternoon she got up from her stool with a very white face and left the shed, walking unsteadily. She never went back to it. She had ceased to be a wonderful woman. It was the very next day that she made David drive her into Melbourne to buy those little odds and ends.

On the way, in the buggy, under a merciless sun, the husband, looking often at his wife, saw at last what manner of changes had taken place. They were outward and visible; they made her look old and ill. It was the worry of recent events, no more, no less. David had been worried himself, he truly said; but there was no sense in anybody's worrying any more about what couldn't be helped, being over and done with, for good and all.

"It's been a bad job," he said again before they got to Melbourne; "a very bad job, as it is. If you let it make you ill, my dear, with thinking about what can't be mended, it'll be a worse job than ever."

He wanted to accompany Mrs. T. upon her unwonted little flutter among the shops. They had put up the mare at their old servant's inn. The landlord had remarked of his former mistress, and to her face, that she was not looking at all well, but, in fact, very poorly. And as David now thought the same, he was very anxious indeed to go with her and hold the odds while she bought the ends. She would not hear of it; but instead of sharply ordering, she entreated him to mind his own business and stay at the inn; so he stayed there, marvelling, for a time. Then a thought struck him.

He went to the pawnbroker's and saw his watch. It was all right. He had it in his hands, and wound it up, and set it right, and listened to its tick as to the beating of some loving heart, while his own went loud and quick with emotion. Then he left, and wandered along the street with eyes that were absent and distraught until they rested for a moment upon a passing face full of misery. He looked again—it was his wife.

They met with a mutual guilty start—hers the guiltier of the two—so that all the questioning came from him.

"Where have you been, my dear?"

"Collins Street."

"And what have you bought, and where is it?"

"Nowhere; I've bought nothing at all. I—I couldn't find what I wanted."

"Not find what you wanted? Not in Melbourne? Nonsense, my dear! You've been to the wrong places; you must take me with you after all. What was it that you wanted most particularly?"

"Nothing, David; I want nothing now. I only want to go home to the farm—only home now, David. There were little things, but—but I couldn't get 'em, and now they don't matter. I am disappointed, but that doesn't matter either. Yes, I am disappointed; but now I only want to get home—to get home!"

She was so disappointed, this tough old woman with the weather-beaten face that was now and suddenly so aged and haggard, that her eyes were full of tears even there in the street; and she let them run over when David forged ahead to push the way; and wiped them up before she took his arm again. This taking of his arm, too, was done more tenderly, more dependently, than ever, perhaps, in their married life before. And David must have felt this himself, for he held up his head and shouldered his way through the crowd like a very brave old gentleman, and drove back to the farm for once the lord and master of his wife—he who had quitted it with less authority than their children.

He was not, of course, exactly aware of it He was conscious of something, but not so much as all that. He did not know enough to keep him awake that night. But the window-blind took shape out of the darkness, and the wife at David's side saw it with eyes that had never closed. And the gray dawn filled the room: and daylight whitened the face and beard of the sleeping man: and the wife at his side raised herself in the bed and looked long upon David, and wept, and kissed the bedclothes where they covered him, because she was frightened of his waking if she kissed him. But he went on sleeping like a child.

Then Mrs. Teesdale lay back and stared at the ceiling, thinking hard. She thought of their long married life together; and had she been a good wife to David? She thought of the easy-going, sweet-tempered young man who had made laughing love to her long ago in some Yorkshire lane; of the middle-aged philosopher who had found it rather amusing than otherwise to watch worse men making their fortunes while he stood still and chuckled; of the frail, white-haired sleeper who would presently awake with a smile to one day more of indolence and unsuccess. She still envied that sweet temperament, as she had envied it when a girl, though she knew now what no girl could have dreamt, that two such natures linked together would have found themselves hand in hand at the poor-house door in very much shorter time than thirty-five years. He had had no vices, this poor dear David of hers. Neither drink nor cards, nor the racecourse, nor another woman, had ever tempted him from their own hearthstone, which was the place he had loved best through all the years. Through all the years he had never spoken a harsh word to wife or child. He was full of affection and incapable of unkindness; but he was equally incapable of making a strong man's way in the world. Therefore she had played the man's part, which had been thrust upon her; and if this had hardened her could she help it? Was it not natural? Hard labour hardens not the hands alone, but the mind, the eye, the face, the tongue, and the heart most of all. It had hardened her; she realised that now, when the strength was gone out of her, and she at last knew what it was to feel soft, and weak, and to need the support which she had hitherto given.

She tried to be just, however. Perhaps the support had not been all on her side through all the years. Perhaps with his even-minded placidity, his unfailing philosophy, David had all along done very nearly as much for her as she for him. Certainly he had never complained, and the life they had led would have been impossible with a complaining man. In their greatest straits he had stood up to her with a smile and a kiss; he had never depressed her with his own depression. That kiss and smile might have seemed impertinent to her at the time, in the actual circumstances, but now she knew how they had helped her by freeing her mind of special care on his account. So after all he had been a good husband to her; nay, the very best; for what other would have borne with her temper as he had done? What other would have been as calm, and kind, and contented? But he was not fit to be by himself. That was the dreadful part of it. He was not fit to be left alone.

To be sure, there were the children. They were still children to their mother, and young children, too; their minds seemed to have grown no older for so many years. Their mother saw the possibility of their marrying one day—as though that day might not have come any time those ten years and more. She saw it still; and what would become of David then? Arabella would not so much matter; she was just such another as her poor father; but John William—

Here Mrs. Teesdale's thoughts left the main track for a very ugly turning indeed. She had taken this turning once or twice before, but it was so ugly that she had never followed it very far. Now, however, she followed it until not another moment could she lie in bed, but must jump up and speak to her son with the matter hot in her head.

It was quite late enough. She was going out a-milking no more, either morning or evening, and that was another thing which John William must be told. Mrs. Teesdale, like everybody else, was glad to have more things than one to speak about, when the one was so difficult, and even dangerous. She partially dressed, and left the room as quietly as possible. The first gray light was penetrating into the passage as she stole along it. When she reached John William's door, there was a noise within; when she opened it, she stood like a rock on the threshold—because she had been a plucky woman all her life—and a man was in the act of getting in by the window.

His middle was across the sill, and the crown of his hat was presented to the door.

"Who are you," said Mrs. Teesdale sternly, "and what do you want?"

The man raised his head instantly; and it was John William himself.

"Holloa, mother!"

"Where have you been?" said Mrs. Teesdale.

"I didn't want to wake you before your time, so I thought I'd come in like this. That's better!"

He landed lightly on the floor; but his feet jingled; he was spurred as well as booted, and dressed, moreover, in his drab tweed suit.

"Where have you been?" said Mrs. Teesdale.

His bed had not been slept in.

"Been? There was something I had to do. No time during the day. So I've just got it done before—"

"Where have you been?" said Mrs. Teesdale.

The young man stared. His mother had repeated the question thrice, each time in exactly the same tone, without raising her voice or moving a muscle as she stood on the threshold, with the brass door-handle still between her fingers.

"What business is it of yours, mother?" he said sullenly. "Surely to goodness I'm old enough to do what I like? I'm not what you'd exactly call a boy."

"You are my boy. Where have you been?"

"In Melbourne—since you so very much want to know."

He had lost patience, and adopted defiance.

"I was sure of it," said Mrs. Teesdale, coming into the room now, and quietly shutting the door behind her. "I was sure of it."

Then, very slowly and deliberately, she raised her left arm, until one lean finger pointed to the wall at his left, and through that wall, as it were, into the room which had been occupied by each of the two visitors. Her eyes flashed into her son's. The lean finger trembled. But she said no word.

"What does that mean?" he asked at last, with an uneasy laugh.

"You have been—with—that woman!"

"I wish I had," said John William.

"You have!" cried his mother.

"I have not. With her? Why, I haven't set eyes on her since the day you took and—the day she left us," said the angered man, ending quietly. "Then what have you been doing?"

"I have been looking for her."

"For that woman?"

"Yes."

"Looking in Melbourne?"

"Yes."

"In the streets?—in the streets?"

"Yes."

"And you have never seen her since—"

"Never."

"But this isn't the first time! You've been looking night after night! So that's why you ran up them other horses? That's why you're half dead unless you get some sleep of afternoons?"

"Mother," he said, "it is."

"Oh, my God!" cried Mrs. Teesdale, reeling, and breaking down very suddenly. "Oh, my God!"

In an instant strong arms were round her; but she would not have them; she freed herself and sat down on the chair that was by the bedside, warding him off with one hand while with the other she covered her face. It cut him to the heart to hear her sobs; to note the tears trickling through the old fingers, gnarled and knotted by a long life of hard work; to see the light strong frame, that had seemed all bone and muscle, like a hawk, so shaken. But because of her other hand, which forbade him to touch her, he could only stand aloof with his beard upon his chest and his thick arms folded. At length she calmed herself; and sat looking up at him with both hands in her lap. Her poor feet were bare; he had snatched a pillow from the bed and pushed it under them while she was still beside herself; and now, when she saw what he had done, she looked at him more kindly; and when she spoke, her voice was softer than ever he had heard it, boy or man.

"John William, you must give this up."

"Mother, we shall break each other's hearts, you and I. I cannot—I cannot!"

"But I know you will. You will give up looking for that girl; you will promise me this before I leave the room. Why should you look for her? How can you expect to find her? You don't know that she is in Melbourne at all. Why should you think of her—"

"Because I've got to think of her, as long as I've a head on my shoulders and a heart in my body."

Mrs. Teesdale had her woman's quick instincts, after all. Hence her very singular omission, on this occasion, to apply a single hard name to the enemy whose deadliest thrust of all was only now coming home to her.

"Very well," she said; "but you must promise to give up looking for her in Melbourne, by night or by day, at any rate while your mother is alive."

"It is all that I can do! It is the only chance!" cried the young man, miserably. "Why should I promise to give up my one chance—"

"Only while I live," interposed the mother.

"But why should I?"

"Because I shall not live very long. Don't look like that—listen to me. I have been ailing for months; never mind how. Whether it was the worry of lately, or what it was, I don't know; but it's only this last week or two that I've felt too poorly to bide it any longer. I never said a word to anybody—I wouldn't have said a word to you—not this morning, but now I must. And you are not to say a word to anybody—least of all to your father—till I give you leave. But the night before last I felt like dying where I sat milking; so I made your father take me into Melbourne, to buy some odds and ends. So I told him, poor man. But a doctor's opinion was all I wanted; that was my odds and ends. And I got it! No, let me tell you first; I went to Dr. James Murray, in Collins Street East. I had heard of him. So I went to him for the worst; but I never thought it would be the very worst; and it was—it was!"

There was an interruption here.

"My boy! Nay you mustn't fret; I'm sixty-three come August, and it's not a bad age isn't that. I may see August, he says. He says I may live a good few months yet. Nay, never mind what it is that's the matter with me; you'll know soon enough. He says he'll come and see me for nothing. It's an interesting case, he says; wanted me to go into a hospital and be under his eye, he did But that I wouldn't, so he thinks he must come and see me. Nay, never mind—never mind! Only promise not to look for that girl—any more—till I am gone."

The promise was given. John William had long been kneeling at his mother's feet, and kissing her hands, her face, her neck, her eyes. That was the interruption which had taken place. Now he was crying like a child.

Mr. Teesdale awoke as his wife reopened their bedroom door.

"My dear," said he, sweetly, "you've been going about with bare feet! You'll be catching your death of cold!"

He was not to be told just yet; and because Mrs. Teesdale's eyes were full of tears, which he must not see, she made answer in her very sharpest manner.

"Mind your own business, and go to sleep again, do!"

David only smiled.

"All right, my dear, you know best. But if you did catch your death o' cold, it'd be a bad job for the lot of us; it'd be the worst job of all, would that!"

CHAPTER XIX

TO THE TUNE OF RAIN

Towards the close of a depressing afternoon in the following winter Arabella might have been seen (but barely heard) to steal out of the farmhouse by the front door, which she shut very softly behind her. Twilight had set in before its time, thanks to the ponderous clouds that were gathered and still gathering overhead; but as she came forth into the open air, Arabella blinked, like one accustomed to no light at all. Rain had fallen freely during the day, but only, it seemed certain, as a foretaste of what was presently to come. At the moment all was very still, which rendered it the more difficult to make no noise; but this time Arabella was not bound upon any secret or private enterprise. She stepped out naturally enough when a few yards from the house, her simple object being a breath of fresh air; and from her white face and tired eyes, of this she was in urgent need. She picked her way as quickly as possible across the muddy yard, but ere she reached the gate was accosted by Old Willie, who was off duty until milk-cart time in the small hours, and who peered at her with a grave, inquiring look before opening his mouth.

"About the same, Miss?"

She shook her head.

"No better, at any rate; if anything, worse."

"And Mr. Teesdale?"

"He is keeping up. The woman who is helping me to nurse has a baby. She had to bring it with her. Father plays with it all day, and it seems to occupy his mind."

"Well, that's something. Now get your snack of air, miss. I mustn't keep you."

"No, you mustn't. I am going to the Cultivation, it is so high and open there. Do you think it will rain before I can get back?"

Old Willie looked aloft. He was an ancient mariner, who had deserted his ship for the diggings in the early days; hence the aptitude for regular night-work.

"I think we shall catch it before pitch-dark," said he; "so you'd better look sharp, miss; and—good-night!"

"Good-night; and thank you—thank you."

But Arabella walked away wincing, and she opened the gate with her left hand; for the horny-fisted old sea-dog had shown his sympathy by nearly breaking her right.

It was the gate that led one among the gum-trees, down into that shallow gully, and so upward to the Cultivation. The trees were as leafy as ever in summer-time; the grass at their feet was much greener. There was no other striking difference to mark the exchange of seasons, saving always the heavy gray sky and the damp raw air. Arabella drew her shawl skin-tight about her shoulders, and walked rapidly; but far swifter than her feet went her thoughts—to last summer.

Heaven knows there were others to think of first—and last—just then. Yet in a minute or two Arabella was thinking only of the wicked, the dishonest, the immoral Missy. Nothing was known of her at the farm from the day she left it. That was nearly eight months ago, and eight months was time enough, surely, to forget her in; but here, of all places, Arabella could never forget the woman who had saved her own woman's honour. Here it had happened. It was at the Cultivation corner that she had made the tryst that would infallibly have been her ruin; it was somewhere hereabouts that Missy had kept that tryst for her and saved her from ruin. She could never come this way without thinking only of Missy, and wondering whether she was alive, and where she was, and what doing. Therefore that which happened this evening was in reality less of a coincidence than it looked.

The girl of whom she was thinking stood suddenly in Arabella's path.

The recognition, however, was not so immediate. Missy was clad in garments that were the meanest rags compared even with those in which she had first appeared at the farm; also, she was thin to emaciation, and not a strand of her distinguishing red hair could be seen for the unsightly bonnet which was tightly fastened over her head and ears. Consider, further, the light, and you will have more patience than Missy had with the dumbfounded Arabella.

"Don't you know me, 'Bella, or won't you know me?"

Arabella did know her then, and her hands flew out to the other's and caught them tight. Then she doubted her knowledge—the hands were harder than her own.

"Missy! No, I don't believe it is you. Where's your fringe? Why are you—like this? How can it be you? You never used to have hard hands!" Yet she held them tight.

"Don't talk so loud," said Missy, nervously; "there might be someone about. You know it's me. I wonder how you can bear to touch me!"

"I can bear a bit more than that," said Arabella warmly, and she flung her arms about the other, and reached up and kissed her lovingly upon the mouth, upon both cheeks. The cheeks were cold, and the back and shoulders were wet to the hands and wrists encircling them.

"You're a good sort, 'Bella," murmured Missy, not particularly touched, but in a grateful tone enough. "You always were. There, that'll do. Fancy you not even being choked off yet—and me like this!"

"Fancy you being back again, Missy! That's the grand thing. I can hardly credit it even now. But you're terribly wet, poor dear! It's dreadful for you, Missy, it is indeed!"

"Oh, that's nothing; it did rain pretty hard, but there'll be some more in a minute, so it would come to the same thing in any case."

"Then you have walked, and were caught in it on the road?"

"Do I look as if I'd ridden? Yes, and it was a pretty long road—"

"From Melbourne?—I should think it was." Missy laughed.

"From Melbourne, that's no distance. I've travelled more than twice as far since morning, my dear, and I shall have it to travel all over again before to-morrow morning."

"Then you haven't come from Melbourne?" cried Arabella, highly amazed.

"Haven't set foot in it since I saw you last."

"Where in the world have you been, then, Missy?"

But even as they were speaking, the grass whispered on every hand, the leaves rustled, and down came the rain in torrents. Arabella found herself taken by the arm and led into the shelter of the nearest tree—a spreading she-oak. She was much agitated.

"Oh, what am I to do?" she cried. "I dare not stay many minutes; but I would give anything to stay ever so long, Missy! You don't understand. Tell me quickly where you have been, if you never went back to Melbourne?"

"Nay, if you're in a hurry, it's you that must tell me things. That's what I've come all this way for, 'Bella—just to hear how you're all getting on. How's Mr. Teesdale?"

"He's as well as he ever is."

"And you, 'Bella?"

"Oh, there's never anything the matter with me."

"And John William?"

"There's not much the matter with him, either."

"Then that's all right," Missy fetched a sigh of relief.

It struck Arabella as very odd indeed that the only one of them after whom Missy did not ask should be Mrs. Teesdale. But was it odd? Quite apart from any rights or wrongs, Mrs. Teesdale had been Missy's natural enemy from the first. Moreover, she had struck Missy as an old woman who would never grow older or die; and Arabella let it pass. She was in a hurry, and it was now her turn to get answers from Missy.

"Where have you been," she repeated, "if you never went back to Melbourne? Be quick and tell me all about it."

Missy shook her head, shaking the rain that had gathered upon her shabby bonnet into Arabella's eyes. It was raining very heavily all this time, and the she-oak's shelter left much to be desired. But Missy was now the one with her arms about the other, who was, as we know, a much shorter woman; so that Arabella, whose back was to the tree-trunk, was being kept wonderfully dry. Missy shook her head.

"I can't tell you much if I'm to tell you quickly. You are in a hurry, I can see, and indeed it's no wonder—"

"Oh, you don't understand, Missy!" cried the other in a torment. "If only you would come into the house—"

"That I never can."

"I tell you that you don't understand. You could—just now."

"Never," said Missy firmly. "I know my sins pretty well by this time. I've had time to study 'em lately; and the worst of the lot was how I played it upon all of you here. Now don't you begin! You want to know where I've been lying low all this while, and what I've been doing. I'll tell you in two twos; then I'll give you what I've got for Mr. Teesdale, and then you shall run away indoors, and back I go to the place I come from. Where's that? Over twenty miles away, in the Dandenong Ranges. It's a farm like this—What am I saying? There never was or will be a farm like this! But it isn't so unlike, either, in this and that; and I'm the girl in the kitchen there, same as Mary Jane is here, and help milk the cows, and cook the dinner, and clean up the place, and all that."

"Oh, Missy, I can scarcely believe it! Yet I felt hard work on your hands the moment I touched them—they are as rough and hard as Mary Jane's," said Arabella, taking fresh hold of them, "and your dress is just like hers. Where did you get such a dress? And how did you come to get taken on at the farm? We all thought you'd gone straight back to Melbourne; as for John William—"

She hesitated. It was one thing to befriend Missy; but Arabella could not help taking a special and a different view of her in relation to her own brother.

"Yes?" said Missy.

"John William was quite sure of it."

"Then—I suppose—he never thought of looking for me? No, of course he wouldn't. Why should he?"

"You—you could hardly expect it, dear, I think," said John William's sister, very gently.

"Hardly; what a cracked thing it was to say!" cried Missy, laughing down the wistful tone into which she had dropped. "But you none of you could have guessed much about my life there, if you thought I was likely to go straight back to Melbourne from here. No, and you can't have known what it was to me to have lived here for two months, even as a cheat and a liar. There's worse things than cheating and lying, 'Bella; there's things that cheating and lying's a healthy change after! But never mind all that. When I left you, and had got through the township, I didn't take the road to Melbourne at all; I took the other road. Bang ahead of me was them Dandenong Ranges that your dear old father's always looking at as he sits at the table. I wonder does he look at 'em as much as ever? So I said, 'Them ranges is the place for me;' and I stumped for them ranges straight away. I swopped dresses with a woman I met on the road; this is the rags of what I got for mine; and then I stopped at all the farms asking for work. How I got work, after ever so long, and all about it, I'd tell you if you weren't in such a hurry to go. You'll get wet, you know, and here you're as dry as a bone. But I suppose it's only natural!"

"It isn't natural, Missy, and it isn't true," said Arabella, earnestly. "Oh, if only you understood everything! As if I could ever forget what you did for me—in this very paddock!"

"It was under this very tree, for that matter," said Missy, with a laugh. "I found it easily enough, and I was standing under it for old acquaintance when you came along. Do you know what he got?"

Arabella hung her head, because in the Argus she had read his sentence, to whom once she had been prepared to commit body and soul. She did not answer; but in her anxiety to be good to Missy, she forgot that other anxiety concerning her brother.

"If only you would come into the house, and let me give you some dry things and some supper! You must need both; and you have no idea how clear the coast is. You don't understand!"

"What is it that I don't understand?" asked Missy, pertinently. "You keep on saying that."

"It is my mother—you never asked after her. She is very ill. She is—on her deathbed."

For more than a minute Missy remained speechless, while the fall of the rain on leaf and blade seemed all at once to have grown very loud. Then she shook her head firmly.

"I am so sorry for you all; but it's all the more reason why I mustn't come in. If she were well, I daren't."

They argued the matter. The want of food was admitted; that of dry clothes, obvious.

"If you would only come as far as the cart-shed; there's not the least chance of anyone going there till Old Willie does at two o'clock in the morning; and there I could bring you some supper and a change as well. If you would only do that," Arabella urged, "it would be something."

"You would promise not to tell a soul?"

"I do promise."

"Not even John William?"

Arabella remembered her forgotten anxiety. "Certainly not John William," said she, emphatically. And Missy gave in at last.

Five minutes later they stood, wet and dripping, in the cart-shed. It was one of the many more or less ramshackle shanties which stood around the homestead yard. It had a galvanised iron roof, a back and two sides of wattle and dab, and no front at all. And no sooner had the two women gained this shelter than a man's voice calling through the rain caused them to cling instinctively together. The man was John William, and, low as his voice was purposely pitched, the words carried clear and clean into the cart-shed.

"'Bella! 'Bella! Where are you, 'Bella?"

And the voice was coming nearer.

"I must go," whispered 'Bella.

"Remember your promise!"

Missy could not know how superfluous was her caution; it comforted her to remember that she had given it, now that she was left alone, able to think, and to examine the situation. This was not that situation which she had planned and bargained for in her own mind; this was the better of the two. She had intended to waylay Arabella, but she had never hoped to manage it so far from the house. She had contemplated the impossibility of waylaying her at all—the necessity of knocking at her window as she was going to bed—the circumstances of a more difficult and a more dangerous interview than that which had already taken place. She knew the daily ways of the farm well enough to know also that she was tolerably safe at present where she was. Soon Arabella would return with eatables and dry clothing, and the one would be as welcome as the other. Meantime, Missy had hidden herself under the spring-cart, lest by any chance another should look into the shed before Arabella. When the latter came back, she would confide into her safe keeping that which she had brought for Mr. Teesdale, to be given him not before Missy had been twenty-four hours gone from the premises. And after that—

Nothing mattered after that.

But Arabella did not return so very soon, after all; and it was uncomfortable for body and nerves alike, crouching under the spring-cart; and the rain made such an uproar on the iron roof that it would be impossible to hear footsteps outside, came they never so near; and this made it worse still for the nerves.

The cow-shed was not far from that which sheltered buggy and carts and Missy in the midst of them. On a perfectly still evening it would have been possible to hear the jet of milk playing on the side of the pail; but to-night Missy could hear nothing but the rain and her own heart beating. It was raining harder than ever. She crouched, watching the sputtering blackness outside until, very suddenly, it ceased to be absolutely black. The light of a lantern came swinging nearer and nearer to the shed.

"What can she want with a lantern?" thought Missy, shrinking for a moment as the rays reached her. Then she extricated herself from the spring-cart wheels, stood upright, and asked the question aloud when the lantern itself was within a yard or two of the shelter. Now you cannot tell who is carrying the ordinary lantern when the night is dark and there is no other light at all; and Missy never dreamt that this was any person but Arabella, until strong arms encircled her and the breath was out of her body.

At last she gasped—

"Arabella told you! She has broken her sacred promise!"

"No one told me; but I saw it in Arabella's face.... Missy! Missy! To think that I have got you safe! I shall never let you go any more—never—never!"

Suddenly he swept her off her feet and bore her into the rain.

"Where are you going to take me? Not into the house?"

She could scarcely speak; she was quite past struggling. Without answering, he bore her on.

CHAPTER XX

THE LAST ENCOUNTER.

It was in the old parlour, an hour later.

Here the change from summer to winter struck the eye more forcibly than it ever can out-of-doors in a country where no leaves fall. The gauze screen which had fitted in front of the fire-place was put away, and a log fire burnt excellently on the whitened hearth; the room was further lighted by the kerosene lamp that stood as of old upon the table; the gun-room door was shut; and a pair of old green curtains, of a different shade from that of the tablecloth, which looked less green and more faded than ever, were drawn across the window.

Mr. Teesdale sat in his accustomed corner, with his chair pushed back and pointing neither towards the table nor the fire, but between the two. On his knee was a bare-legged child, perhaps fourteen months old. Arabella, when she was in the room, took a chair near the table, if she sat down at all, and the lamplight only blackened the inscription of sleepless nights and anxious days that was cut deep upon her pallid face. John William sat at that end of the sofa which he had invariably affected, watching Missy; they all did this, even to Mr. Tees-dale, who was also occupied with the child upon his knee; but all save the child, who sometimes crowed and was checked, sat more like waxworks in a show than living, suffering beings.

When one spoke, it was in a whisper. But there was very little speaking. If Missy had not come back at all they could scarcely have been more silent.

Yet the way they spoke to her when they spoke at all—the way they looked at her, whether they spoke or not—this was much more remarkable than their silence, for which there was good reason. They spoke to Missy as to an old and valued friend, who had come at a cruel time, but who brought her own welcome even so; they looked at her with hospitable, grieved eyes that entreated her to take the kindly will for the kindlier deed. Across their faces, too, there now and then swept looks of apprehension which she did not see; but never a shade that would have led a stranger to suspect that they knew aught but good of this girl, or that she had rendered aught but kindness to them and theirs.

As for Missy, she did not see half their looks, because her own eyes had been either averted or downcast during the whole of the hour that she had already spent in the room. Now they were averted. She was sitting on a stool by the fireside—by that side of the fire which was furthest from Mr. Teesdale and nearest to the door. Her body was bent forward; her eyes were fixed pensively upon the fire; her left elbow rested upon her knee, and her chin in the hollow of her left hand. Hand and face were brown alike from hard work in all weathers. It was the weather of that day, however, that had quenched the colour from her hair; limp and soaking as it was, it looked much less red than formerly in the glare of midsummer. Also the fringe had disappeared entirely; but this alteration was permanent. Most notable of all changes, however, was the gauntness and angularity of the old good figure, which had struck Arabella even in the darkness; it was painfully conspicuous in the light. Missy had been to her box with Arabella, and was clad in a blouse and skirt that had been made for her ten months earlier. They fitted but loosely now. A hat and jacket, which she had also obtained from her box, had been taken away from her by John William: it lay within reach of his hand upon the sofa, where he appeared content to sit still and stare fixedly at Missy's back. Thus he was not aware that she had taken a small roll of papers out of her blouse, and that her right hand had been for some time fidgeting with it in her lap. And when David, who had a much better view, broke the silence with a low-toned question, the younger Teesdale had to get up in order to understand what his father meant.

"What is it you have got there, Missy?"

"It is something that I—I wanted to talk to you about, Mr. Teesdale." She turned her head and looked a little wistfully at John William and Arabella; but neither of these two perceived that she wished to speak to Mr. Teesdale alone; and, after all, there was no reason why she should not speak out in front of them.

So she proceeded. "It's something rather important—it's the only thing that could ever have brought me back here. Mr. Teesdale, you never took possession of my box after all!"

"'Twasn't likely," said David.

"But I meant you to. I told Arabella—"

"Yes, yes, but you didn't really and truly expect me to take you at your word, Missy?"

"Of course I did. The box was yours. It and all that was in it had been bought with your money."

"I wouldn't have anybody touch the box," said David, with characteristic pride. "I took and locked it up myself, and I've kept the key in my pocket ever since."

"But it was all yours by rights—"

"I care nothing at all about that!"

"The dresses and things, as well as the box itself, were worth something. Not much, perhaps—still, something. And then there were four pounds and some silver which I'd never touched. Here they are—four pounds."

She got up and laid them in a row on the tablecloth under the lamp. The others had risen also; and John William, for one, had his eyes fixed upon the little roll of paper in her right hand. It was a roll of one-pound notes. She began to lay them one by one upon the table, counting aloud as she did so.

"One, two, three, four, five, six—"

"Stop a moment," said David, trembling. "How did you come by them, Missy?"

"Seven, eight. Didn't I tell you that I've been working all this time upon a farm? Nine—"

"Ah, yes, you did."

There had been a few explanations—a very few—when John William had first brought her in. Then dry clothes, then supper, then silence. It must be remembered that the shadow of death hung over the farm.

"Ten. I was there thirty-three weeks last Saturday. Eleven. They gave me ten shillings a week, and they found me—twelve—in food and clothes. I had things to put up with—thirteen—but nothing I couldn't bear. I was thankful you'd taught me to milk here. Fourteen, fifteen. I was so! Sixteen, and that's the lot. Sixteen and four's twenty. Twenty pound I got out of you, Mr. Tees-dale, because I couldn't resist it when you said what you may recollect saying as you drove me back into Melbourne that first day. I never meant to pay you back; I wasn't half sure that I'd ever let you see me again. I don't say I should have done it if I'd known you'd go and pawn your watch for me; still I did do you out of the twenty pounds, and I meant to do you out of them for good and all. But here they are."

"Thank you, Missy," said David at last. The others said nothing at all.

"Thank me! I don't want you to thank me at all. What have I done but rob you and pay you back again? No—I only want you—to forgive me—if you can!"

"I do forgive you, my dear; but I forgave you long ago," said David, smoothing back her hair and kissing her upon the forehead.

"You two forgive me, I know," she said, turning to the others.

Arabella embraced her tearfully, but John William only laughed sardonically. What had he to forgive?

"I knew you did. So now there is only one thing more that I want to send me away happy."

"Send you away! Where to? You've only just come," cried Mr. Teesdale, as loud as he dared; but even as he spoke he remembered the special difficulty of the occasion, and his face twitched with the pain. "Why, where did you think of going to?" he added, wiping his lips with his red pocket-handkerchief.

"Back to the Dandenong Ranges. I'm so happy there, you don't know! Thought I'd left? Not me, don't you believe it. No, I must get back to my work as quick as I can. And you'll be able to sit in quietness and look out through the gun-room window"—she pointed to the gun-room door—"and across the river-timber to them blue ranges, and you'll be able to say, 'Missy's working there. She's honest now, whatever she was once; and she's trying to make up for her whole life.' Yes, and you may say, 'She's trying to make up for it all, and it was us that taught her; it was us that took her out of hell and gave her a glimpse of the other thing!' That's what you'll be able to say, Mr. Teesdale. And I'll know you're looking at the ranges, and I'll think you're looking at me, every evening in the summer-time, and every dinner-time all the year round. They ain't so blue as they look, when you get there—I guess the sky isn't either when you get there—but they're blue enough for Missy; they're blue enough for me."

The tears were running down her face. John William had interjected, here and there, "You're never going back at all." But she had taken no notice of him; and when he repeated the same speech now, she shook her head and only sobbed the more.

"What is it that would send you away happy?" asked poor David; for he knew well what the answer was to be; and by now he was himself intensely agitated.

"I want someone else to forgive me, too," said Missy, "if it is not too late." And she looked at the door that led into the passage that led to Mrs. Tees-dale's room. This door, also, was kept carefully closed.

"It is too late for you to see her; it would not be safe," said Mr. Teesdale, sadly shaking his head. "But she lies yonder at peace with all mankind; she has told me so herself. Rest assured that she forgives you, Missy."

"She would forgive you with all her heart," said Arabella. "She has been so brave and good—and gentle—ever since she first fell ill. She would forgive you, Missy, as freely as my father has done."

"She has forgiven you long ago," declared John William. "She spoke to me about you the morning after she had been to see the doctor without telling us she was going. She spoke of you then without any bitterness; so she had forgiven you as long ago as that."

Missy received these optimistic assurances with a look of dissatisfied doubt, as though she could accept no forgiveness that was not actual and absolute. Then her eyes found their way back to the passage door; and she could scarce believe them. She sprang backward with a cry of fear. The other three started also with one accord—so that the room shook. For the door was open, and on the threshold, like a spectre, stood none other than the dying woman herself.

"Forgive you!" she said, in a crazy rattle of a voice. "You!"

She entered without stumbling, shut the door behind her, and took two steps forward. They appeared the steps of a decrepit, rather than a dying woman; but they brought her no nearer to Missy, who backed in terror towards the gun-room. Nor was poor Missy worse than any of the rest, who not one of them could put out a hand to uphold this tottering, terrible figure, so scared and shaken were they. And the old woman stood there in her bedclothes, with a ghastly dew upon her emaciated face, and ordered the young girl out of the house.

"Forgive you!" she said. "Go; how dare you come back? David—all of you—how dare you take her in—a common slut—with me on my deathbed? How long have you had her here, I wonder? Not long, I know, or I should ha' felt it—I should ha' known! Do you think I could have died in my bed with that—with that in the house? God forgive you all; and you, out you go. Do you hear? Go!"

She pointed to the gun-room door with a bony, quivering hand; and because the girl she abhorred was paralysed with horror, she brought that hand down passionately upon the table, so that the four sovereigns rang together, and she saw the gold and notes, and fiercely inquired where they came from.

But now at last David was supporting her in his arms, and he answered soothingly:

"They are twenty pounds that Missy borrowed from me when she was with us—I never told you about it. She has come to-night and paid them back to me. That's the only reason she is here. She has been all this time earning them, just to do something to atone."

"Pah!" cried Mrs. Teesdale, stiffening herself in her husband's arms, and reaching her skinny hands to the notes and gold. "How came you to have twenty pounds to give her? How comes she to have them to give you back? How do you think she earned them? Shall I tell you how?" the poor woman screamed. "They're the wages of sin—the wages of sin—of sin!" She snatched up gold and notes alike and flung the lot at the fire with all her feeble might. The gold went ringing round the whitened hearth. The notes fell short.

"Now go," she said to Missy, her scream dropping to a whisper, "and come back at your peril."

Missy got her hat and jacket from the sofa, brushing the wall all the way, and never taking her eyes from that awful, menacing, death-smitten face. Then suddenly she plucked up courage, took one step forward, and stood in profound humility, mutely asking for that forgiveness which she was never to get. A strong hand, young Teesdale's, had laid hold of her arm from behind and given her strength.

David, too, was putting in a quavering word for her.

"She is going," said he. "She was going in any case. You are wrong about the money. She has earned it honestly, as a farm servant, like our Mary Jane. Can't you see how brown her face and hands are? We have all forgiven her, as we hope to be forgiven. Cannot you also forgive her, my dear, and let her go her ways in peace?"

The sick woman wavered, and for a moment the terrible gaze, transfixing Missy, turned, by comparison, almost soft. Then it shifted and fell upon the bearded face of him who was supporting the unhappy girl, and moment, mood and chance were gone, all three, beyond redemption.

"John William," said his mother, "leave her alone. Do you hear me? Let her go!"

Nothing happened.

"Let her go!" screamed Mrs. Teesdale. "Choose once and for all between us—your dying mother and—that—woman!"

At first nothing; then the man's hand dropped clear of the girl.

"Now go," said the woman to the girl.

The girl fled into the gun-room, and so out into the night, only pausing to shut the doors behind her, one after the other. With the shutting of the outer door—it was not slammed—they heard the last of Missy.

"Now follow her," said the mother to the man.

But the man remained.

CHAPTER XXI

"FOR THIS CAUSE"

Now there was nothing but wet grass between the gun-room window and the river-timber; and that way lay the Dandenong Ranges; therefore it was clearly Missy's way—until she stopped to think.

This was not until she had very nearly walked into the Yarra itself; it was only then that she came to know what she was doing, to consider what she must do next, and to recall coherently the circumstances of her last and final expulsion from the farmhouse of the Teesdales. Already it seemed to have happened hours ago, instead of minutes. The hat and jacket she had snatched up from the sofa were still upon her arm; she put them on now, because suddenly she had turned cold. Another moment and she could not have said on which arm she had carried them, she had carried them so short a time. Yet the deathly face and the deathlier voice of Mrs. Teesdale were as a horror of old standing; there was something so familiar about them; they seemed to have dwelt in her memory so long. But, indeed, her mind was in a mist, through which the remote and the immediate past loomed equally indistinct and far away.

The mist parted suddenly. One face shone through it with a baleful light. It was the dreadful face of Mrs. Teesdale.

"Dying!" exclaimed Missy, eyeing the face judicially in her mind. "Dying? Not she—not now! She may have been dying; but she won't die now. No, I've saved her by dragging her off her deathbed to curse me and turn me out! I've heard of folks turning the corner like that. She was right enough, though. You can't blame her and call her unkind. The others are more to blame for going on being kind to one of my sort. No, she'd better not die now, she'd much better leave that to me."

Her mind was in a mist. She tried to see ahead. She must live somewhere, and she must do something for her living. But what—but where?

There was one matter about which she had not spoken the truth even now; neither to Arabella, nor to John William, nor to Mr. Teesdale himself. That was the matter of her new home in the Dandenong Ranges, where she said she had been so happy, they didn't know! It was no home at all. She was particularly wretched there. She had stayed on with one object alone; now that this was accomplished there would be no object at all in going back. She had not intended ever to return, when leaving; but then her intentions had gone no further than the paying back to Mr. Teesdale of the twenty pounds obtained from him once upon a time by fraud. This had been the be-all and end-all of her existence for many months past. It was strange to be without it now; but to go back without it, to that farm in the ranges, would be terrible Yet go somewhere she must; and there was the work which she could do. They would give her that work again, and readily, as before; they would overwork her, bully her, speak hardly to her—but clothe her decently, feed her well, and pay her ten shillings a week, all as before. She must do some work somewhere. Then what and where else?

Her mind was in a mist.

She saw no future for herself at all, or none that would be tolerable now. If she had dreamt once of unanimous forgiveness at the farm—of getting work there in the kitchen, in the cow-shed—that dream had come to such utter annihilation that even the memory of it entered her head no more. And she wanted no work elsewhere. So why work at all? She had done enough. Rest was all she wanted now. It was the newborn desire of her heart; rest, and nothing more.

And here was the river at her feet; but that thought did not stay or crystallise just yet.

Before it came the thought of Melbourne and the old life, which parted the mind's mist with a lurid light. That old life need not necessarily be an absolutely wicked one. There were points about that old life, wicked or otherwise. It had warmth, colour, jingle and glare, abundant variety, and superabundant gaiety. But rest? And rest was all she wanted now—all. And the mist gathered again in her mind; but the river still ran at her feet.

The river! How little heed she had taken of it until this moment! She had watched without seeing it, but she noted everything now. That the rain must have stopped before her banishment from the house, since her dry clothes were dry still; that overhead there was more clear sky than clouds; that the clouds were racing past a sickle moon, overwhelming it now and then, like white waves and a glistening rock; that the wind was shivering and groaning through the river-timber, and that it had loosened her own hair; that the river itself was strong, full, noisy and turbulent, and so close, so very close to her own feet.

She stooped, she knelt, she reached and touched it with her fingers. The river was certainly very cold and of so full a current that it swept the finger-tips out of the water as soon as they touched it. But this was only in winter-time. In summer it was a very different thing.

In summer-time the river was low and still and warm to the hand; the grass upon the banks was dry and yellow; the bottle-green trees were spotted and alive with the vivid reds, emeralds, and yellows of parrot, parrakeet, and cherry-picker; and the blue sky pressed upon the interlacing branches, not only over one's head but under one's feet, if one stood where Missy was standing now and looked where she was looking.

She was imagining all these things, as she had heard and seen and felt them many a time last summer. Last Christmas Day was the one she had especially in mind. It was so very hard to realise that it was the same place. Yet there was no getting over that fact. And Missy was closer than she knew to the spot where she had cast herself upon the ground and shut out sight and hearing until poor John William arrived upon the spot and brought about a little scene which she remembered more vividly than many a more startling one of her own unaided making. Poor Jack, indeed! Since that day he had been daily in her thoughts, and always as poor Jack. Because he had got it into his head that he was in love—and with her—that was why he was to be pitied; or rather, it was why she had pitied him so long, whom she pitied no longer. To-night—now, at any rate, as she stood by the river—of the two she pitied only herself.

To-night she had seen him again; to-night he had carried her in his arms, but spoken no word of love to her; to-night he had stood aside and allowed her to be turned out of the house by his mother who was not dying—not she.

It was as it should be; it was also as she had prayed that it might be. He did not care. That was all. She only regretted she had so long tormented herself with the thought that he might, nay, that he did care. She felt the need of that torment now as keenly as though it had been a comfort. Without it, she was lonely and alone, and more than ever in need of rest.

Then, suddenly, she remembered how that very day—last Christmas Day—in the gorgeous summer-time, but in this selfsame spot—the idea had come to her which was with her now. And her soul rose up in arms against herself for what she had not done last Christmas Day.

"If only I had," she cried, "the trouble would have been over when it seems it was only just beginning. I shouldn't have disgusted them as I did on purpose that very afternoon. A lot of good it did me! And they would all have forgiven me, when they found out. Even Mrs. Teesdale would have forgiven me then. And Jack—Jack—I shouldn't have lived to know you never cared."

She clasped her hands in front of her and looked up steadily at the moon. It was clear of the clouds now—a keen-edged sickle against a slatey sky; and such light as it shed fell full enough upon the thin brown face and fearless eyes of the nameless girl whom, as Missy, two or three simple honest folk had learnt to like so well that they could think of her kindly even when the black worst was known of her. Her lips moved—perhaps in prayer for those two or three—perhaps to crave forgiveness for herself; but they never trembled. Neither did her knees, though suddenly she knelt. And now her eyes were shut; and it seems, or she must have heard him, her ears also. She opened her eyes again, however, to look her last at sky and moon. But her eyes were full of tears. So she shut them tight, and, putting her hands in front of her, swung slowly forward.

It was then that John William stooped forward and caught her firmly by the waist; but, after a single shrill scream, the spirit left her as surely as it must had he never been there.... Only, it came back.

He had taken off his coat. She was lying upon it, while he knelt over her. The narrow moon was like a glory over his head.

"Why did you do it?" she asked him. "You might have let me get to rest when—when you didn't care!"

"I do care!" he answered; "and I mean you to rest now all the days of your life—your new life, Missy. I have cared all the time. But now I care more than ever."

"Your father and 'Bella—"

"Care as much as I do, pretty nearly, in their own way. Missy, dear, don't you care, too,—for me?"

She looked at him gratefully through her starting tears. "How can I help it? You picked me up out of the gutter between you; but it was you alone that kept me out of it, after I'd gone; because I sort of felt all the time that you cared. But oh, you must never marry me. I am thinking so of your mother! She will never, never forgive me; I couldn't expect it; and she is going to get quite better, you know—I feel sure that she is better already."

He put his hand upon the hair that was only golden in the moonshine: he peered into the wan face with infinite sadness: for here it was that Missy was both right and wrong.

E. W. Hornung – A Short Biography

Ernest William Hornung was born on 7th June 1866 at Cleveland Villas, Marton, Middlesbrough. He was the third son, and youngest of eight children, to John Peter Hornung and his wife Harriet née Armstrong.

By the age of 13 Hornung had joined St Ninian's Preparatory School in Moffat, Dumfriesshire before enrolling at the exclusive Uppingham School, in Rutland, in 1880.

Hornung suffered from a general state of bad health, including asthma and poor eyesight but managed to be well-liked at school and to develop a life-long passion of cricket. He loved to play despite the obvious fact that his talents were rather limited.

At 17 his health worsened, and he left Uppingham to travel to Australia, where a sunnier climate was deemed to be better for his various ailments.

Upon arriving he worked as a tutor to the Parsons family in Mossgiel, in New South Wales. As well as teaching he spent time working in remote sheep stations in the outback and began to contribute materials to the weekly magazine; The Bulletin. It was also at this time that he began work on his first novel.

After two years of very valuable life experiences Hornung returned to England in February 1886, a few months before the death of his father, in November, whose deteriorating business interests had become a constant worry.

Hornung found work in London as a journalist and story writer. In 1887 he published his first story under his own name, 'Stroke of Five', which appeared in Belgravia magazine. His work as a journalist coincided with the reign of terror brought about by Jack the Ripper's grisly murders. From this Hornung developed an interest in criminal behaviour.

He had completed the manuscript of the novel he brought back from Australia and, between July and November 1890, the story, 'A Bride from the Bush', was published in five parts in the respected Cornhill Magazine. It was released later that year in book form. This, his first novel, was well received by critics.

Hoping to further his talents in cricket Hornung, in 1891, became a member of two cricket clubs: the Idlers, whose members included Arthur Conan Doyle and Jerome K. Jerome, and the Strand club.

Hornung knew Doyle's sister, Constance ('Connie') from when he had visited Portugal. Connie was described as attractive, "with pre-Raphaelite looks ... the most sought-after of the Doyle daughters".

They were married on 27th September 1893, although Doyle was not at the wedding and relations between the two writers were occasionally difficult. The Hornung's had their only child, a son, Arthur Oscar (but always called just Oscar), in 1895.

In 1894 Doyle and Hornung began work on a play for Henry Irving, on the subject of boxing; Doyle was, at first, eager to begin and paid Hornung a £50 advance but then withdrew before the first act had been completed: the play was never finished.

Like Hornung's first novel, 'Tiny Luttrell' had Australia as a backdrop and the device of an Australian woman in a culturally alien environment. This theme ran through his next four novels: 'The Boss of Taroomba' (1894), 'The Unbidden Guest' (1894), 'Irralie's Bushranger' (1896), in this Hornung introduced the character of Stingaree, an Oxford-educated, Australian gentleman thief. In 'The Rogue's March' (1896) Hornung began to show a growing fascination with the motivation behind criminal behaviour and was sympathetic to the criminal hero as a victim of events. It was different thinking but caused some consternation for others.

In 1898 Hornung's mother died and he dedicated his next book, a series of short stories; Some Persons Unknown, to her memory.

Later that year Hornung and Connie spent six months in Posillipo, Italy. An account of this trip was published in the May 1899 issue of the Cornhill Magazine.

The fictional character Stingaree was re-written to become his most famous creation; A. J. Raffles; the gentleman thief, first used in six short stories published in 1898 in Cassell's Magazine. Modelled on George Cecil Ives, a Cambridge-educated criminologist and talented cricketer who, like Raffles, lived in the Albany, a gentlemen's only residence in Mayfair. The first tale of the series 'In the Chains of Crime' was published in June that year, titled 'The Ides of March'.

Another account adds to the richness by asserting that Raffles and his sidekick, Bunny Manders, were based not only on Doyle's Holmes and Watson but also on his friends Oscar Wilde and his lover, Lord Alfred Douglas. Whatever the exact amalgam the characters were warmly embraced by the reading public who turned it into both a popular and financial success, although some critics echoed Doyle's own fears of the dubious nature of a criminal being used as a hero.

In early 1899, the Hornung's returned to London, and resided in Pitt Street, West Kensington, for the next six years.

After publishing two novels, 'Dead Men Tell No Tales' (1899) and 'Peccavi' (1900), Hornung published a second collection of Raffles stories, 'The Black Mask', in 1901. The critics again complained about the criminal aspect. The public who bought them had no such qualms.

In 1903 Hornung collaborated with Eugène Presbrey to write a four-act play, 'Raffles, The Amateur Cracksman', which was based on two previously published short stories, 'Gentlemen and Players' and 'The Return Match'. The play was first performed at the Princess Theatre, New York, on 27th October 1903 and ran for 168 performances.

In 1905, after publishing four other books in the interim, Hornung brought back the character Stingaree. Later that year, in response to public demand he published a third collection of Raffles stories in 'A Thief in the Night', in which Manders relates some of the earlier adventures he had had with Raffles.

In 1909 the final Raffles story was published, the full-length novel 'Mr. Justice Raffles'. It was poorly received. The Observer reviewer asking if "Hornung is perhaps a little tired of Raffles".

It seems not. That same year he partnered with Charles Sansom for the play 'A Visit From Raffles', which was performed in November that year at the Brixton Empress Theatre, London.

Hornung turned away from Raffles thereafter, and in February 1911 published 'The Camera Fiend', a thriller whose narrator is an asthmatic cricket enthusiast and his attempts to photograph the soul as it leaves the body. This was followed by 'Fathers of Men' (1912) and 'The Thousandth Woman' (1913) before 'Witching Hill' (1913), a collection of eight short stories in which he introduced the characters Uvo Delavoye and the narrator Gillon. In 1914 his fictional works ceased with 'The Crime Doctor'.

His son, Oscar, left Eton College in 1914, and was due to proceed to King's College, Cambridge later that year. However, the terrors of WWI were about to unleash themselves all over Europe. Oscar volunteered, and was commissioned into the Essex Regiment. He was killed, aged a mere 20, at the Second Battle of Ypres on 6th July 1915.

Although heartbroken Hornung edited and issued privately a collection of Oscar's letters home under the title 'Trusty and Well Beloved', in 1916.

Around this time Hornung himself joined an anti-aircraft unit. He also joined the YMCA and did volunteer work in England for soldiers on leave. In March 1917 he visited France, writing a poem about his experience afterwards—something he had been doing more frequently since Oscar's death—and a collection of his war poetry, 'Ballad of Ensign Joy', was published later that year.

In July 1917 Hornung's poem, 'Wooden Crosses', was published in The Times, and in September, 'Bond and Free' appeared. A few months later he was accepted as a volunteer in a YMCA canteen and library just a few miles behind the Front Line.

Hornung was concerned about support for pacifism among troops and wrote to Connie about it. She spoke to Doyle and, rather than discussing it with Hornung, he informed the military authorities. Hornung was naturally angered by Doyle's action and relations between the two men were further strained as a result. He continued to work at the library until a German offensive overran the British positions and he was forced to retreat, firstly to Amiens and then, in April, back to England. He stayed in England until November 1918, when he again took up his YMCA duties, establishing a rest hut and library in Cologne.

In 1919 Hornung's account of his time spent in France, 'Notes of a Camp-Follower on the Western Front', was published. Doyle later wrote of the book that "there are parts of it which are brilliant in their vivid portrayal". That year Hornung also published his third and final volume of poetry, 'The Young Guard'.

Hornung finished his YMCA work and returned to England in early 1919. He worked on a new novel but was hampered by poor health. But Connie's was of greater concern. In February 1921 they took a holiday in the south of France to recuperate. Whilst travelling there on the train Hornung fell ill with a chill that progressed to influenza and finally pneumonia.

Ernest William Hornung died on 22nd March 1921, aged 54.

He was buried in Saint-Jean-de-Luz, in the south of France, in a grave adjacent to that of George Gissing.

E. W. Hornung – A Concise Bibliography

Periodicals
Stroke of Five (1887, Belgravia)
Spoilt Negative (1887, Belgravia)
Nettleship's Score (January 1890, Cornhill Magazine)
A Bride From the Bush (5 Parts. July-Nov, Cornhill Magazine, 1890)
Thunderbolt's Mate (4 Parts. March 1892, Chambers's Journal)
Kenyon's Innings (April 1892, Longman's Magazine)
The Burrawurra Brand (November 1893, The Idler)
The Unbidden Guest (6 Parts. May-Oct 1894, Longman's Magazine)
The Governess at Greenbush (4 parts. February 1895, Chambers's Journal)
After the Fact (3 Parts. January 1896, Chambers's Journal)
The Ides of March (June 1898, Cassell's Magazine)
A Villa in a Vineyard (May 1899, Cornhill Magazine)
No Sinicure: More Adventures of the Amateur Cracksman (January 1901, Scribner's Magazine)
A Jubilee Present: More Adventures of the Amateur Cracksman (February 1901, Scribner's Magazine)
The Fate of Faustina: More Adventures of the Amateur Cracksman (March 1901, Scribner's Magazine)
The Last Laugh: More Adventures of the Amateur Cracksman (April 1901, Scribner's Magazine)
To Catch a Thief: More Adventures of the Amateur Cracksman (May 1901, Scribner's Magazine)

An Old Flame: More Adventures of the Amateur Cracksman (June 1901, Scribner's Magazine)
The Wrong House: More Adventures of the Amateur Cracksman (Sept 1901, Scribner's Magazine)
Chrystal's Century (June 1903, Atlantic Monthly)
Charles Reade (June 1921, London Mercury)

Novels and Short Story Collection

A Bride from the Bush (1890) Novel
Under Two Skies (1892) Short story collection
Tiny Luttrell (1893) Novel; two volumes
The Boss of Taroomba (1894) Novel
The Unbidden Guest (1894) Novel
Irralie's Bushranger (1896) Novel
The Rogue's March: A Romance (1896) Novel
My Lord Duke (1897) Novel
Some Persons Unknown (1898) Short story collection
Young Blood (1898) Novel
The Amateur Cracksman (1899) Short story collection
Dead Men Tell No Tales (1899) Novel
The Belle of Toorak (1900) Novel; published in the US as The Shadow of a Man
Peccavi (1900) Novel
The Black Mask (1901) Short story collection; republished as Raffles: Further Adventures of the Amateur Cracksman
At Large (1902) Novel
The Shadow of the Rope (1902) Novel
Denis Dent: A Novel (1903) Novel
No Hero (1903) Novel
Stingaree (1905) Novel
A Thief in the Night (1905) Short story collection; republished as A Thief in the Night: Further Adventures of A. J. Raffles, Cricketer and Cracksman
Raffles: The Amateur Cracksman (1906) Short story collection; stories taken from The Amateur Cracksman and The Black Mask
Mr. Justice Raffles (1909) Novel
The Camera Fiend (1911) Novel
Fathers of Men (1912) Novel
The Thousandth Woman (1913) Novel
Witching Hill (1913) Short story collection
The Crime Doctor (1914) Short story collection
Old Offenders and a Few Old Scores (Published posthumously) Short story collection

Plays

Raffles, The Amateur Cracksman (27th October 1903) By Hornung and Eugéne Presbrey; first performed at the Princess Theatre, New York
Stingaree, the Bushranger (1st February 1908) First performed at the Queen's Theatre, London
A Visit From Raffles (1st November 1909) By Hornung and Charles Sansom; first performed at the Brixton Empress Theatre, London

Non-Fiction

'Trusty and Well Beloved', The Little Record of Arthur Oscar Hornung (1915) Privately published
Notes of a Camp-Follower on the Western Front (1919)

Poetry
Ballad of Ensign Joy (1917)
Wooden Cross (1918)
The Young Guard (1919)